"Magic and mystery reside in *American Canyon*—a place where the ancient meets the contemporary, and where the profane becomes sacred. In this elegant volume, Ravva composes provocative narratives of devotion and defiance that remind us that we are all migrants in mind and memory."

-- VARUN SONI

"*American Canyon* is a book like none I have encountered, an almost hallucinatory immediacy offered with rare generosity. Ravva's tapestry of East and West demonstrates the importance of remembering rituals and histories—those of both personal and social scale."

-- NANCY BUCHANAN

"A mesmerizing and elegiac meditation on identity, nationality, and desire. Ravva coils narratives of India and the American West in on each other, telling a family history that is both fragmented and tender. A phenomenal debut."

-- COLIN DICKEY

American Canyon

A:M:A:R:N:A:T:H   R:A:V:V:A

KAYA PRESS
LOS ANGELES

Published by Kaya Press (Muae Publishing, Inc.)
www.kaya.com

For information about permission to reproduce selections from this book,
please write to permissions@kaya.com.

Designed at The Royal Academy of Nuts + Bolts, D.O.D.
www.TheRoyalAcademy.org/DOD

Distributed by D.A.P./Distributed Art Publishers
155 Avenue of the Americas, 2nd Floor, New York, NY 10013
800.338.BOOK   www.artbook.com

LIBRARY OF CONGRESS CATALOGING-IN-PUBLICATION DATA
Ravva, Amarnath.
    American Canyon / by Amarnath Ravva.
        pages cm
    ISBN 978-1-885030-16-0 (pbk. : alk. paper)
    1. Ravva, Amarnath. 2. Authors, American--21st century--Biography.
    3. East and West--Biography. 4. Mothers and sons--Biography.
    5. Literature, Experimental. I. Title.
PS3618.A946Z46 2014
814'.6--dc23   [B]   2013048295

23 22 21 20 19 18 17 16 15 14   10 9 8 7 6 5 4 3 2 1
Printed in China

This publication is made possible by support from the USC Dana and David
Dornsife College of Arts, Letters, and Sciences; the USC Department of
American Studies and Ethnicity; and the USC Asian American Studies Program.
Special thanks to the Choi Chang Soo Foundation for their support of this work.
Additional support was provided by the generous contributions of Lisa Chen &
Andy Hsiao, Floyd Cheung, Susannah Donahue-Negbaur, Sesshu Foster, Lillian
Howan, Qing Lan Huang, Keesoo Huh & Jisun Suh, Bill Lee & Corey Ohama,
Whakyung & Hong Yung Lee, Ericka Matluck, Minya & Yun Oh, Lily So &
Tom Beischer, Duncan Williams, Amelia Wu & Sachin Adarkar, Anita Wu &
James Spicer, Patricia Miye Wakida, Amy Zeifang, and others.

To Amina
and to Farrell

In every culture, in every place and time, there has always been a religion, and in every one of these religions there has always been the gesture of bowing so fully that the forehead strikes the ground.

—Lew Welch

karma

---

retribution

Ravi yells, *Don't go too far into the water—it's deep and the stones are slippery!*
At the top of the steps, he is looking through the viewfinder of the
video camera. He works in Pamban at a hydroelectric plant and was
sent to help me because I don't know Tamil, the language spoken
on this island off the coast; Ravi, who grew up in Andhra Pradesh,
knows both Tamil and Telugu. I stop two steps from the edge and
place my glasses on a dry patch of stone. The first step is green, from
algae, and slides under my foot. I steady myself. The mandapam at
the center of the tank bears the eroding couplets of the Thirukkural
above the water.

The water stains the edge of my towel green. I splash it three times at my face. There is no way I will put my head under this water. There isn't even a lotus flower in the tank. I know millions of Hindus have done this before me. Here. At this very tank. Their dirt floats before it settles. I turn around to see Ravi approach the water's edge. He gestures for me to immerse myself. I take another step further down, close my eyes, and dunk my head. I do this three times because of tradition, and one more time, just in case.

THERE IS A WAY to begin a ritual. You first talk to a guide, who introduces you to a pujari, who then approaches the superintendent of the temple services. We skip these steps because Ravi's boss knows the superintendent. He says we have to be discreet. Everyone takes their share. Signs posted on the stone blocks of the passageway inside are in Tamil and English: "No non-Hindus allowed inside the temple." They are very strict here in Rameswaram; even Sonia Gandhi had to request permission to enter, though she was the wife of the prime minister at the time—born in Italy, she was not Hindu by birth, but had converted. The superintendent, whose office is next door to the temple, assigns me a head priest and takes 10,000 rupees.

At night, I return to the hotel, where my friend from Berkeley, Chris, is recovering from a cold. I tell him about my interaction with the superintendent, and he says, *The spectre of your uncle follows us wherever we go in India.* My uncle, a financial consultant for power projects, mostly hydroelectric, has a developed network of contacts which includes Ravi's boss. In the third bed, next to Chris', Ravi silently reads the paper. Before I entered his life, Ravi would sit down to eat at home, his idlis covered in sambar, his son lost in the folds of his wife's sari. At the hotel, the amount of pickle he uses reflects how much he hates the food.

YESTERDAY I FOUND OUT the exact time I was born and told the pujari. Another pujari, across the bridge in Pamban, produced my birth chart with his computer. They discussed the details. Where the stars shone when I was born. How they rested in the sky. They determined over the phone that there was no reason for me to do the naga prathista, but if I was going to go through with it, I first had to wash away the misfortune of being born in America with the waters of the Lakshmana Tirtham.

MORE THAN A THOUSAND YEARS AGO in the Dandak forest, Ravana's uncle Maricha used his maya to become a doe to lure Rama and Lakshmana away from Sitha. When he pranced through their encampment, Sitha called out to her husband. *Look! What a beautiful doe. See how it shines in the sunlight, gently nibbling on grass? Can you catch it? Please? I'll die without it!* Lakshmana cautioned his brother: *It must be a demon, because no deer could be made of gold with jewels in its hide.* To which Rama replied, *Haven't you heard of the seven golden swans? Who are as real as you are? The world is full of wonder. If it is real, I will capture it; if it is a demon, then it will die by the shafts of my arrows!* Rama was led deep into the wood before one of his arrows found its mark. The doe fell onto the dark leaves that littered the forest floor and cried out in his voice. *Lakshmana, please help me!*

Left alone, Sitha prayed for her husband's safe return. She might have closed her eyes. Or they were covered in tears. In Ravana's flying vehicle, the Pushpaka Vimanam, she couldn't watch the woods disappear into the earth below. Would he have abducted her if he had remembered the curse? Four yugas before, he had tried to steal Vedavathi from her husband, Vishnu, in a forest much like this one. He had grabbed her long black hair; Vedavathi cut it. He had reached for her arm—which turned into fire. Before she immolated the rest of herself, Vedavathi cursed him. *I will be born again to destroy you,* she said. *I will be born from the earth.*

Months later, when Hanuman led the brothers to rescue Sitha, they stopped at Rameswaram. They took a bath in this tirtham.

In Ravana's garden, Sitha waited under a Sorrowless Tree coming into bloom.

THE PREVIOUS WINTER, Ammamma came from India to help my mother, who was sick. Her doctors weren't sure of the cause—complications from giardia from Lake Tahoe years before was one possibility, while another was that her immune system was inflaming her colon because of a bacteria or virus. Ammamma didn't think that that was why her daughter was sick. It was a symptom of the spirit, not the body. She decided to consult her seer, who was in India, by phone.

He helped them. The seer. But the title she addressed him with, Sharma, is really another name for someone like the pujari sitting before me next to folded silk cloth. Each piece has a use in the naga prathista that is never arbitrary, but rather an expression of balance and order. When doctors look at an x-ray, or when Sharma in meditation gazes at the idea of my mother, they see an expression of another magnitude, an image of uncontrolled energy or a dark mass, a reddening or flash of useless heat.

That summer, Ammamma and my mother returned to India, where my mother's health recovered. In Benicia, we speculated on reasons why. Now that her children had left, she felt lonely. My sister and father pointed their fingers at the heart. I pointed to nature. Exxon, half a mile away, burned orange over the hills.

IN RISHIKESH, the sky is split with its own light. From the ghat, our flames drift down the river at dusk. The sadhus' robes cover the steps in orange, and they sing and clap their hands in unison. Their robes were once white. All around them is the smoke of their pyre.

AT THE TRIVENI GHATS, I meet Ganesh, a sadhu who says he draws strength from walking by the water at sunset. Around us, people are gathering to release their deepums, little flames floating in ghee, down the Ganga. The river tumbles out of the mountains, clear with patches of green like the Feather River coming out of the canyon near Chico, California. We see a man lean down and drink water in the cups of his hands, and Ganesh turns to me and says:

See how much faith he has? He thinks it is safe to drink the water because it is holy. I would never drink the water here. I saw wild elephants last summer on the other side amongst the trees. They always drink where the water moves fast enough. So do I.

IN HYDERABAD. I receive my first email from a sadhu. It comes from an internet cafe's general email account—fast@sikkanet.com. I call the phone number in the message and ask the lady who answers, *Is Ganesh Puri there?* She says, *No, there is no Ganesh Puri here,* and angrily hangs up the phone. Odd. I call again, and this time he answers.

EARLIER THAT SUMMER, I had discussed Arundhati Roy's thoughts on big dam projects with my uncle, who's worked in the power sector for more than a decade. Her book, *The Greater Common Good*, had influenced me; I wondered what he thought of her points. He told me that without harnessing a reusable energy resource such as water, India would have never become an industrialized nation. He felt Roy's activism, like her recent protest outside the Supreme Court building and subsequent jailing, had been fueled by an impossible desire to attain reparations for the millions of people dispossessed by the Narmada Valley Project. But the government just didn't have the resources. A weak argument, I thought, considering the billions spent to displace them in the first place. My uncle suspected the motives of others. And he could not discount the horrors of mega dams, what Nehru called the "Temples of a Resurgent India." He believed in smaller hydroelectric projects that harnessed the flow of river water with small turbines instead of the use of dams and levees to turn them into lakes. His most recent project had been in Sikkim, a protected area of the western Himalayas, where the earth reaches into the sky and pulls out a river, drop by drop.

ONCE, I READ A STORY in the newspaper about a herd of wild elephants. Their forest had been chopped down by developers, so they left to live in another one north of Delhi. Years later, the elephants heard the echo of trees falling again. They recognized the yellow bulldozers. But this time, as the developers slept, the elephants dragged all of their equipment and threw it off a nearby cliff.

KNOWING IT does not matter. The forests were quiet when my father began to study the effects of DDT in the soil in the late '70s. On his bookshelf was *Silent Spring* by Rachel Carson, and after reading it, I asked him how he could still approve of pesticide use. *Without DDT*, he replied, *millions would have died from malaria*.

I open my eyes to reflections of palm trees holding their green fruit. The water has the salty taste of the ocean. It bloats the cotton around my waist with weight. I walk past the video camera and disappear into the world it can't see. I try to change discretely but drop my towel, and Ravi yells "chi-chi" in embarrassment. A family of seven, with their backs turned, face a pujari with a cream shawl split by a green stripe thrown over his shoulder. They perform the rites for the death of a family member, repeating what he says in Sanskrit. They say this tirtham is that strong. It can cleanse away death. As I dry, the sky grows blue around them.

WHEN I WAS YOUNG, there were always two trips we would take. The kids would pile into the car and Krishna, my uncle's company-provided driver, would take us to the ruins of Golconda Fort eight miles outside of Hyderabad. The city within its walls had once glittered from the trade of diamonds, giving birth to the Koh-i-Noor, the Hope, and the Orloff. We would run among the rolling hills near the outer walls and dodge the flocks of goats watched over by shepherds sitting on rocks. The ruins of the fort tower over the Deccan Plateau it once ruled. Its stones are covered by moss.

On the way back, I would stare at Krishna's hands as they turned the steering wheel. A picture of Jesus Christ hung from the rearview mirror. Krishna's left hand had two thumbs like a distant cousin of Ammamma's I had once met. His genes had come together to produce his hand, and descendants of his might also have hidden inside the walled nucleus of their cells, in the alleles of their chromosomes, this same mix of genetic history. His trait will show like a facet cut in stone.

On a hill in the middle of the city shone the white marble of the Birla Temple, the other place we would often visit. On such trips, everyone would go. One Sunday morning, I refused. I told them I didn't believe in God. My uncle called in Thathayya to deal with the adolescent atheist. He approached, armed with a branch of green leaves. *Why don't you believe in god?* he asked. *It's irrational. God can't be proven,* I replied. He held up his branch. *Can you explain how this simple leaf works?* Its thin skin revealed a network of tunnels and paths. I couldn't. I hadn't learned about chlorophyll or mitochondria. *No matter how smart we are, scientists still can't explain how a leaf works. Does that mean they don't exist, don't thrive in our gardens, don't continue to grow?*

FOR FOUR YEARS, Ganesh has lived on water and a glass of milk a day. When he has a guest, like me, he drinks a bottle of coke. When the rain comes, he stops drinking water and gathers moisture from the air. He tells me with a hint of jealousy that NASA is studying another sadhu like him, who they keep under constant surveillance. *There is a scientific explanation,* he says. *It would let us travel through space.* Ganesh invites me to do the same; he would like me to videotape his every moment as he performs his yearly pilgrimage to Rameswaram.

GANESH STAYS in a bare room with blue trim, a green mat, three books, a picture of his guru, and a metal glass for water. His room overlooks an alley wide enough for a rickshaw that leads down to the ghat. Mr. Nagi lives in a small room at the bottom of the stairs next to the toilet and cooks bland food. He provides Ganesh with his daily glass of milk out of devotion.

I place my setup in the far corner of the room to get his entire body in the shot. He tells me that video cameras sap his energy and only allows me to tape him on the third day of our talks.

Is it better to know or not know? I ask him. He leans back, letting his hair refract bits of sun.

Was it a year ago? I think it was two. Yes. Two years. The whole world. Not just your United States of America. Even a poor country like India. Accentuating

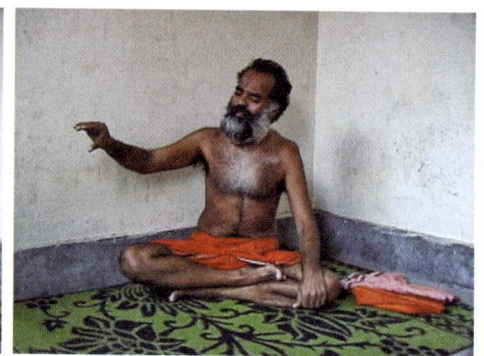

each word, he gesticulates the imaginary headline of a newspaper. *Every day the headlines. Bill Clinton and Monica L-oo-winsk-ii? Monica Lewinski. They had this, they talked this, they got together at so and so place, so and so. Not a day, not two days, not a month, but the whole year! That was also news, knowledge?* I murmur affirmatively. *It is knowledge! But for me it is of no use. I think for many people around the world it is of no use. What Bill Clinton did to Monica Lewinski? Was it true? Or not true? Or even, to what extent they went?* He points at the grey hair on his chest and adjusts the cloth around his waist. *What difference does it make to me? Has it changed the lives of many people, the knowledge of the whole year, those headlines? Of course certain people made lots of money from that type of news and that type of knowledge. But for most people, it didn't change their lives. It didn't bring anything good to anyone's life. What use is it to me? For me it is a burden. That type of knowledge is useless to me. It's even harmful to me. I want to go into a state where my mind is at peace. The function of this type of knowledge is contrary to what I want to achieve. It will take me in another direction.*

As I told you, I was an electrical engineer. I worked in the Indian Navy and after that I worked in the Merchant Marines. I've been around the world. That knowledge, of electrical engineering, helped me when I was in that field, in my previous life, you can say. But it is no use to me now. How much do I need to know? He points up at the ceiling, *I do not need to know how that fan motor works,* then points at the far corner, *or how your camera works. Yes, I knew all those things. But at this stage, it is of no use to me.*

I REMEMBER how, when I was seven, Ammamma used to take me to sing bhajans with all the other grandmothers in a hall in Markapur. The hall was part of an old house and connected to the temple by a corridor, I thought, because it was so close to one of the temple's four gates. I imagined a secret door traversed by pujaris in their orange cloth. The stone floor and walls were polished from years of old round ladies singing and clapping, from the coconut oil in their greying hair. The pillars around them lent them grace.

When a sodi came by, she would strum a metal wire attached to a gourd while looking at their palms. They would take turns hearing her sing the song of their hands. At that age, I thought she was a fortune teller with a musical instrument, a gypsy like the ones who came by for food and had tiny mirrors sewn into the fabric of their clothes like patches of light shining through the diamond lattice of a trellis.

The sodi is a spirit medium. She sees spirits through the body's cracks. Skeptics say she is more like a village journalist who knows all the gossip, having heard it during her morning rounds. She will remember when you ask her to tell you your story, stretching the palm of your hand towards hers.

IN 1983, I was sweating in the shade of a sky blue room. On the floor was a small jumping spider, rubbing its head with its front paws. I watched him for a while; he was suspicious, keeping his eight eyes at all times on what he thought was moving. I listened to the old black circular fan at Pedda Attha's house in Podili, the town where my father grew up. Above me, and standing out sharply from the background of the wall, was a picture of a lightly mustached man, someone I had never met. Pedda Attha grew tired when she looked at her son. Her daughter, Radhika, took me up to the flat cement roof with piles of mud along its seams to stop the rain from leaking inside. She wore an orange red petticoat and matching ribbons wrapped in her black hair. Her smile was perfect, one of her dimples darker than the other.

I LISTENED to the rain as it fell mid-day that summer in August. I slept next to my grandfather, who reeked of Chivas Regal whiskey and 555 cigarettes. Thathayya had very little hair on his body, which he prided himself on, saying in his animated hours that he had "baby soft" skin.

I remembered how we had travelled to Thathayya's—the bus had honked its way out of Hyderabad through rural stops, through towns with white plastered temples, through streets lined with fruit carts and hot burning corn and had played chicken with other buses on one-lane highways in the heart of Andhra. It was packed after an hour of this; a baby perched on the haunch of a woman standing next to my seat pissed all over my shoes and legs, and the mother insisted that I should sit in my mother's lap because I was young enough for it. Twelve hours later, we crested the hills down into Markapur, past the reservoir and into the main center, where Thathayya greeted us through the window and took us home.

When I opened my eyes, I heard wet clothes tied in bundles and slapped dry against a rock outside. A rickshaw with a bullhorn pedaled by, announcing the latest movie, one with Sridevi and Kamal Hassan. Everything was audible because Thathayya's house was over a sari store on the main street full of stray dogs and dust clouds from passing trucks and the foot-pedal sewing machine of a tailor that whirred at the bottom of the stairs by the front door. Up above all of this noise was the roof, where I slept when it was dry; from there I could stare at the blue to black sky through the mesh of the mosquito net over my bed at night.

When I came down from the roof to go to the outhouse, I passed my grandmother, Ammamma, sifting rice for dinner. Nearby, a pile of cooked rice from the night before was being picked at by blackbirds. My grandmother was still young. She had married T. Chennakesavulu when he was twenty-four and she was thirteen.

T. Chennakesavulu, or Thathayya, was the surviving son of seventeen; all his brothers and sisters had died before they were seven. His father had bought all the land on the main street and watched its value go up as it became the business section of town. In Thathayya's house, the only thing left of his father was an iron blue safe the size of a fridge and a picture of him, one eye covered by a black patch. I liked to pull on Thathayya's ears, elephant ears, and he told me that there were rabbits inside his stomach that needed to be fed, which is why he drank so much.

When Thathayya went out to the club in his see-through shirt, the smell of cards in the air, he sometimes took me with him, and I would look at the India Times, the only magazine there in English. Usually he would run out of cigarettes. Then he would call me over, pull out a ten rupee note, brown with Ashoka pillars on one side and a Bengal tiger on the other, and tell me to get a pack of GoldFlakes or sometimes 555 said like "Five-Fifty-Fives." The other gamblers, each with their own Ray-Ban style glasses and graying facial hair, all claimed that Thathayya had built the club.

I saw pictures of him carrying a gun in the jungles of Srisailam. He used to hunt tigers, played a good game of chess, and was state tennis champion when he was young. Sometimes he would come home from the club with fireworks hidden behind his back to surprise me with, and I would take them up to the roof to blow out of bottles, watching the clouds burst with their stars. All the kids in the neighborhood would hear the whistle of the rockets crack the air and hop from one roof to the next until they reached mine and then stand around, laughing and taking their turns.

One night, I woke to the sound of a woman screaming across the street. In the shapes across the road I could see her sitting down with her foot stretched out, and heard some men saying that a black scorpion had stung her. I remembered how my uncle used to crunch the ones that slept in the middle of the pavement under his boot when we would walk home from the midnight matinee.

When Thathayya would come home for his midday nap, he would pull out a matchbox with a lotus flower on the front and place it against the wall, quickly opening the box to release a little white scorpion. It would run in frightening circles around the room, moving around from one wall to the other until it came back to the place where it had begun. He said that it could kill a grown man, but this one had its stinger cut off. When I wasn't looking, he would grin and make a scorpion's stinger by placing all of the fingers of his right hand over each other in a segmented arc, then reach over and sting me.

When he finished his Chivas Regal, he would drop a match in the bottle to show the flame ball up inside.

WE, THE KIDS on the roof. My cousin Radhika tells me about her homework for the day. In her hand is a diagram, a biological illustration of a dragonfly, two hatch-marked eyes laid flat on the page. Why do they make her memorize this? She doesn't ask that question herself. Her younger brother wants to go see Podilamma. He jumps up and down announcing where she is. Radhika's eyes are large, like squat almonds. She looks towards where her brother points and says, *Yes*. She is a little older and guides us. At the back of the shrine are two figures. One is beautiful, wearing a silk sari; behind her is another figure, the first Podilamma, made by her brothers, who couldn't afford better than the rough rock with silver eyes. Slivers of sunlight make them glow; at night, they reflect our rotating wicks, our small bundles of incense. We become reverent for a few seconds before we jitter out of the temple.

TEN YEARS LATER, THATHAYYA, my grandfather, has found his way into my family's living room in California. He is the figure of loss. When it rains, he sits in a chair in the garage next to the minivan and smokes cigarettes. In good weather, he follows the cardiovascular jogging route in the park down the street until his cigarette is finished.

The pujari lives in a two-story building a few hundred yards away from the temple, across the street from an internet cafe that has no internet. He greets us at the front door and motions for us to go in. The front room is empty except for a square pit at one end for the fire of the puja. He hands me a chart, and I realize that they have typed in my name as "rama" born in "newyark u.s Saint Helena" instead of "amar" born in "ithaca, new york, u.s." The longitude and latitude are off by a few degrees, and they have managed to reverse my name. These are not my stars. They belong to someone else or no one at all. The pujari tells me to change in the back of the house into the clothes I've bought for the ceremony—a pair of cotton pants, like pajamas, and a pancha, which is a wide scarf that covers your upper body. I wash my feet and hands with a small brass pitcher and watch the dirt from the tirtham flow down a small channel into the open sewer that runs under his front doorstep, carrying a black effluent to the ocean. Where did this water come from? There is no well to be seen behind his house. The water under the island is full of salt.

IN FRONT OF OUR TEMPLES or the doors of our houses are swirls of muggulu. They invite what is welcome inside. On Fridays, at dawn, hands stitch the earth together. They begin with a grid of evenly spaced dots to guide them and to maintain symmetry. If they are young, they carefully produce straight lines and gentle curves. If older, they render a design that shows their practice, or one that shows disinterest. They use chalk, or white flour, and sometimes add a touch of yellow or orange.

On religious holidays, they will bring out the rare and expensive colors—purple, blue, green, red, occasionally brown or a golden yellow—and create the design they had fallen in love with when they were younger. They will fetch some dung and mix it in a bucket with water and prepare their canvas by moistening the earth with it.

Now their colors will be brighter and their images will keep their form, keep the shape of their flowers and leaves when faced with wind.

Before, when there were no roads, this dark water was antiseptic. We spread it on our fields to let our food grow strong. We washed our floors with it—no more than bare ground—to kill germs.

We walked along the seams of the earth made by oxen.

Our wheels were wood.

OUTSIDE THE TEMPLE IN PODILI stands a chariot, taller than all of our houses, which took years to build. An artist carved myths in rows along its sides, telling each story with thousands of figures until he reached the end of the line. He was dwarfed by the large wheels that carried his myths around town once a year. He chiseled in their shadows.

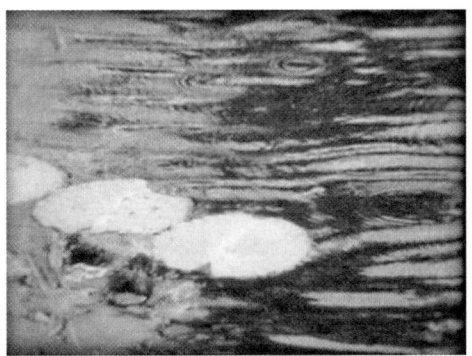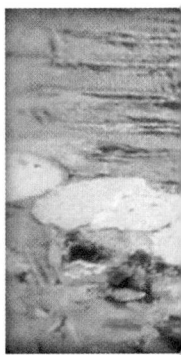

He lays out nine brass vessels. The largest, surya, is in the middle, with the other eight in a square around it—chandra, kethu, rahu, shani, shukra, brihaspati, budha, mangala. His wife and his mother sleep in the back room, and the smell of the seashore, the odor of a thousand wet dogs, is absent. He applies three red kum kum lines, eyes, to each of the vessels, then fills them with rice. Earlier, his wife had drawn a muggu with white rice flour on the floor, which spirals out from underneath the sun and the planets.

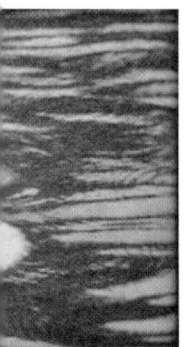

WE WERE ALWAYS reconstructing India within the confines of America. Past the parking lot lay land separating us from the families of Silicon Valley. When the shilpies arrived to this hollow space on the developer's map, the neighbors had no idea what they were cutting out of stone. As it rose, piece by piece, they saw a tall white tower unlike any church. It was a piece of India, exact in all dimensions, that had been brought over in each of the shilpies' minds. The neighbors watched from their kitchens and made calls to the Livermore city offices. They wished for the emptiness to return and grow its weeds.

Attached to the lot was a temporary temple. A small, modest three or four bedroom model, ranch style, in a shade of greenish brown. At night, the shilpies slept on the beige carpet. They dreamt of home.

For a moment, the pujari climbs upstairs. At the end of the next room is a ladder that stretches up into the dark space above our heads. A space from which descendants climb down after talking to their ancestors. When he was born, verses were handed down to him along with a packet of clothes. A name was waiting for him. Each of its syllables mapped out his life's task. It taught him to wash his hands frequently and to never touch meat. *You are purity. Teach this to the others*, it said. *Never leave.* When he comes back, I see he has several pieces of silk cloth in his hands, which he places on the floor next to him.

WHEN I WAS SIXTEEN, Ammamma made me a ring out of a set of nine jewels she had inherited from her mother. *Each stone is a symbol for each of the nine planets including the sun,* she said as she pointed out their black statues at the temple in Markapur. These were the navagrahas she visited every day. Their faces radiated out, with a larger one, the sun, in the middle of the square the rest made around him. On the plane home, I tapped the ring on the metal armrest while listening to music and bent it out of shape. The gold was pure enough to be soft. It slipped from my finger and never touched the earth. I never heard it fall.

She said the temple was born out of the earth. Five hundred years ago, Krishnadevaraya built the gopuram and outer structures that still hide parts of the town in their shadows. She liked to tell me stories about the ancient ruler as if he were a famous actor she saw on the street.

In Krishnadevaraya's court were eight poets—astadiggajalu—who were like elephants. One of them was Vi-ka-ta-ka-vi. He stumped many with his riddles and wit, as his name suggests—it is a palindrome of the word kavi, or poet.

When Vikatakavi was young, he saw a Kalika Devi temple along the road and went inside. Silently, he asked her all the questions he had, which impressed her. She wrote a beeja aksharam, or letter, on his tongue. This gave him the gift of poetry, and he immediately praised her. Flattered, she decided to give him another gift and held out two bowls. *One bowl will give you wealth, and the other bowl will give you knowledge. Choose one.* He took both bowls, mixed them together, and drank.

In response to her rage, he said that he wanted both. She laughed. *Who would do such a thing. You will have your vidya and you will make money, but it will never stay with you. Since you made me laugh, that is what you will be remembered by.*

AMMAMMA REMEMBERED WHEN her husband was the rich man she had married. On either side of her stood houses they once owned that she had watched slip out of his hands. All that was left was the jewelry she wore the day she sat in the kalyana mandapam and a rain-soaked sack on the roof. Inside was a paper trail of property tax documents from the beginning of the century to independence. Each had a British stamp with the image of the sovereign, King George or Queen Anne, and I always hoped to stumble upon the first stamp ever made, the "penny black." I spent that summer learning the subtle differences of their faces and the shades of color they wore. I dreamed that the hundreds of colors I saved in an album turned black. Halfway through the bag, I stopped searching and left it on the roof to swell with each monsoon. I let their carmine faces fade under the sun's pressure. Let water dissolve the royal insignias that could only be seen when they were held up to the light.

The pujari is young and has no beard. His name is Chandra. He tells me to sit on a straw mat along the blue wall of the room. The muggu is abstract, unlike the ones made of leaves and flowers around Podili, and is composed of lines, circles, and crescents. Chandra places a different colored piece of fabric on each vessel and covers them with flowers. To my left is a rock the shape of a cobra's hood that I have seen before propped up against the trunk of a tree in town, or along a road, or in a temple courtyard. Carved on its surface are two entwined cobras stained yellow with pasupu; they resemble the caduceus of Hermes, the symbol of medicine for western hospitals and pharmacies. To the ancient Greeks, this was a symbol of the occult, of alchemy. Chandra tells me that this ceremony is performed for women who can't have children. That is what the prathista can heal; the barren womb. What effect will it have on me? As I sit here, the document, the video, is creating itself. Like an orchid's stalk growing out of red bark, every hour a new segment arrives, and at the end, when it becomes still, is a green bud.

YEARS BEFORE, or generations later, depending on who you are, my mother hits her head and says "na karma!" which means "my fate!" I am watching the Discovery channel and she is frying samosas. *What do you mean?* I ask. When she is at a loss for the right word, or tired, or has doubts about her son, she speaks in Telugu. The burden of what lies between us becomes mine. The samosas are almost ready; I enter the kitchen and listen to what she says. Behind me, a bald eagle feeds her young on a cliff somewhere in America.

You know your thathayya was a fool. He never worked a day in his life, and look at us now, all of us have to work hard. All he did was gamble away his money, and when he needed to pay for something, like putting his kids through school, he sold a house. Now look, he has nothing, not even his own house. He's been renting that for a year now. A couple of years ago, he took all the money he had left and built the only three-star hotel in Markapur. It cost him twenty lakhs! Yesterday, Mamayya called and said that Thathayya got really drunk with his partner, someone he trusted. He had him sign a paper, saying that it was a government document for the hotel, to keep it under regulations. It turned out that your grandfather had signed away the whole hotel to this man, twenty lakhs! Now he has nothing! But when his father died, there were bad omens. It's a custom to put rice outside overnight as an offering to a father's spirit, to make sure that his soul is content. The blackbirds never ate the rice. They didn't even touch it.

TWO YEARS AGO, my mother's seer handed me a piece of lined paper my grandmother had torn out of a notebook. It was off-white with faded blue lines, wide rule, for the ease of children learning how to write. He asked me to mark some dots on it. Anyway I wished. After he had looked at their arrangement for a few minutes, he went into a trance. His nose twitched. I had a hard time believing in him, but my mother, and her mother, and her mother's mother never had any doubts about him, or his father, or his father's father.

He said I have a naga dosham, like Nayanamma. Unlike karma, which is the fruit of what your soul did in its previous life, a naga dosham is the result of prarabdha karma. Prarabdha karma is the fruit of your actions during this life. It is immediate retribution.

01:40:00:15

At the beginning of a ceremony there are always three questions. *What is your name?* Amarnath. *What is your gothram?* Nabella. *What is your nakshatram?* Rohini. Rohini is red, is Alpha Tauri. Nabella is another name for family. Amarnath is a cave in the Himalayas, is a piece of paper encased in gold around my neck, is the ice lingam which forms deep inside away from light, is the site of Indian, Kashmiri, and Pakistani strife, is a pilgrimage up a mountain never safe enough for my ascent. The steps that follow are repeated; a chant and the echo of that chant. Sound for sound. Even if I can't pronounce the line or go too slow, I must throw flowers on the navagrahas for each one. They are my words, my sounds. They will fall from my mouth as well as my hands.

OUR TRAIN is speeding across the Deccan Plateau heading towards Hyderabad. In the compartment next to me are old soldiers in their eighties described as freedom fighters by a young man who says he is a politician. His friend, a grandson of one of the soldiers, tells me about his home in Warangal.

Do you know why India has remained whole after all of these years? How we can speak different languages and continue to call each other Indian even though we can't understand each other? My mother, when she went down to the Godavari, near Warangal, to do her ceremonies, she called it Ganga. This is why we understand each other. All of our rivers are Ganga.

Every September, we take clay sculptures of the god Ganesh down to the water of the San Francisco Bay and return him to his home. At the bottoms of rivers and oceans in India there are millions of elephant-headed bodies of half-eroded clay left by families over the years. Underneath the foot of the Golden Gate Bridge, ours have begun to crumble.

01 : 45 : 00 : 00

In these moments between the endless chain of flowers, I think of the mothers who placed me here without any order or discernible reason. I've watched them bless silver, gold, and brass with devotion. Inside myself, like fire, are their stories. Inside these moments, I ask them questions with no answers because the chain stretches from before I breathed and spoke.

WHEN WE DO THE HOMAM, my mother brings a gold chain with a dangling bar that is hollow inside, called a thayathu, with her. When she called I said *Yes*, even though I didn't think of myself as very religious. *How long will it take?* I asked. If she had answered, she would have said, *All day.*

Inside, the floor is covered with carpet. I had expected stone. The courtyard around the sanctums is enclosed as a concession to the neighbors.

We chant a shloka and then offer ghee to the fire 1001 times. It burns in the square pit covered with tin foil, giving us smoke and heat in return. Its flicker is reflected in the pujari's glasses, which are as thick as an old bottle that has washed up. The tide's reiterations, like our chants, recede away from land and towards its own dark heart, a trail of shells and eddies in its wake.

By the end of the homam, sweat has collected on our skin. The pujari writes my name in Sanskrit on a piece of paper and grabs some ashes from the dying fire. He seals them inside.

When my mother puts the thayathu around my neck, she says it will ward off Shani, or Saturn. She tells me to never take it off.

EVERY YEAR, the lines under my eyes grow more visible. The planets shift their positions through the night sky, exerting a different effect on all of us below. We are pulled by invisible threads. To predict their paths and the pull of these threads, physicists supply us with equations. In the East, Sharma has his visions. He gathers charts and maps around him.

Sharma can see rivers inside our bodies. Two curve up our backs and form the hood of a cobra. They race to meet each other like a body approaching its reflection in the mirror. But when the two lack balance, they lose their symmetry—reflections arrive late, or sometimes not at all. When Sharma looked at me from thousands of miles away in the landscape of his visions, he saw more than imbalance. My snake was asleep. Sharma told my mother the homam in Livermore would bring me back into symmetry by awakening it.

In one of Chris' books—*The Serpent Power*, a description of yoga written in the 1920s by Sir John Woodroffe—is a picture of two channels of energy, the pingalā and the idā, which form the hood of a serpent. They traverse up, parallel, from the kidneys to the neck. One of them is a channel of fire. Yogis spend years learning how to manipulate them.

He makes sure I throw the stems too. A car honks on the street; his baby screams from the back of the house. The flowers form questions in heaps. I have no answers.

The pujaris have grown in number, emerging from the midday sun into the shade of our room to shelter the ritual with their bodies, each one wrapped in the red cloth of their profession. They focus on the task at hand, the prathista, which must be finished without pause. These are the hours when we are vulnerable, when chance can put an end to the necessary order of our movements. One of them asks about the video camera and Ravi repeats what I had told him earlier, except in Tamil. My mother left India three months ago, before the dry season began. The wind kicks up dust where she stays with her brother in the center of town, which aggravates her lungs. Ravi tells them the videotape is for her.

WHEN MY MOTHER returned from India, she pointed at the house, at history. Do we know who lived here before? She asked if any Native Americans lived in this part of California, in Benicia, on this hill. She knew I had gone to the Maidu Bear Dance on the third weekend of June, just before the summer solstice. The Indian American had met the American Indians in the Sierras and found some kinship.

Why was she asking about Benician history? She would rather buy a new tract home over an old Victorian, and through rituals and the burning of spices, through wall hangings that narrated myths, through the planting of her thulsi plant that is always found around houses in India, she would make it her own.

TWO DAYS AGO, the trip from Chennai to Rameswaram had been on a narrow gauge track. We never went fast and rocked back and forth like a boat in the ocean. Between one cabin and the next, a door, blue on the inside, dull red on the outside, opened to a stream of rice paddies dotted with palm trees. It left rust on our hands. When we bent along a curve, the hot air mixed with soot. Under the bridge, I saw sand the color of the sun.

YESTERDAY, I WATCHED the boats in the ocean from the roof of the hotel. Their sails lined the horizon in red, white, and blue. Their wood slid past the water around them gently. The wind blew until they vanished. Closer, by the beach blackened by sewage, a man searched for empty water bottles and dogs barked. Behind them, the fishing boats twirled in circles held by chains that wouldn't let them go.

IN 1988, my father lay in his own sweat and heat in an empty house in America. The doctors said he had malaria. Mosquitoes around the house he had grown up in and visited that summer with me had left behind reminders on our skin. He made sure I had quinine after dinner every day because he knew my body wasn't used to India, wasn't used to its germs and parasites. We lay on the roof in the night surrounded by them.

His back ached as he dreamt of the first time he had gone back to India since leaving. The town had erected a tent outside the movie theater so they could ask him questions; he was the first to have left Podili for America.

As his fever increased, the air around him grew cold. He was no longer the returning son he had once been. He remembered the constant ring of the phone in his father's store that summer when he had met his four possible wives. He knew he could only marry my mother. They both knew the first time they met. I have a picture. They are on the roof and the wind is blowing.

(HOURS):(MINUTES):(SECONDS):(FRAMES)

At some point in your life, the seer says, *your shadow fell upon a snake in the forest.*

maya

---

illusion

I AM LYING IN BED when I hear a song from the Ramayana. By the time I wake up, it is gone, and my nephew is trying to attract my attention.

"Sandeep," I ask, "did you hear the people singing this morning?"
"Yes, Mamayya, I heard them."
"Do you know where they are? Do you think we can find them?"
He nods.
"Are you sure?"
Another, less certain nod.
"Let's go," I tell him.
"But why, Mamayya?"
"I want to videotape them."

His eyes light up. He likes to dance in front of the camera. I can involve him in the process and edit out his antics later, if I have to. For the next hour, I follow him around town. He doesn't know where they are, but I know we will find them begging for alms up the street from Pedda Attha's husband's fertilizer and pesticide shop. One of them is clearly Rama; his blue face is framed by hair that curls out from underneath a gold crown. The other, with round monkey cheeks and a tail poking out of his pancha, is Hanuman. I stretch out my hand, full of change, and shake my camera while Sandeep, though he doesn't have to, translates my excitement into words the singers understand.

Like Rama in exile, they wander the earth acting out a story they have inherited. At night, crouched next to their bundles of masks and tails, they will chat with others who stop to sleep under a temple's stone roof—yogis, pilgrims, and mystics. Some are born into this existence; others have renounced their former lives for this one. They are points in motion connecting one stone platform to another. One town to the next.

RAMA AND HIS ARMY OF MONKEYS reached the shore of the southern sea. They uprooted mountains, rocks, and hillocks; they piled sand and dirt until their work was done. Groups of monkeys tied their tails around hills and tossed them into the water. On the third day, a bridge reached Lanka's beaches. Rakshasas said to each other, *Look! The sky holds the sand out of the ocean.* Ravana's capital, burnt by Hanuman's fiery tail weeks before, continued to smolder in the distance. Groves of sandalwood and akhil had turned to ash; the gold used to pave the city's floors had melted into pools in the ocean.

In a small temple near the Lakshmana Tirtham are the relics from this bridge. In the center of a cement tank float two large pieces of smooth coral that have broken off an underwater reef. The pujari pushes the floating pieces into the tank. *See how they float? This is how Rama's army crossed the sea. They used these magic rocks!*

AFTER PICKING ME UP at the BART station, my sister asks in the car, "It's Rakhi tomorrow. Will you stay in town so I can tie a rakhi on you?"

"Yeah, but I have a lot of work to do," I reply, looking at the rows of condominiums hidden behind thin patches of eucalyptus. Rakhi is the day when your siblings and cousins tie bracelets—purple and glittery, or sometimes red and shiny gold—around your wrist; in return, you promise to protect them and give them a present. For me, the rakhi would be tied around the wrist of my bāva or an elder sibling if I had one. I asked my mother once who my bāva was since I didn't have an older brother, and she told me that he was my cousin who had died a long time ago, the year I was born.

A couple of months after you were born, we went back to India. Everyone wanted to see you, so we went everywhere so they could. When we were in Podili, your bāva was going to school in a hostel about 10 kilometers outside of town. He was studious, like your father. He really wanted to see you, so he left at night in a hard rain. He didn't see the electric wire that had fallen on the road during the storm.

PEDDA ATTHA ALWAYS SAYS that I am like my bāva, her son that I never met. In Podili, everyone has to step over open sewers to get to their front door, and the temple next door to us has broken shards of bottles stuck into the top of the cement walls so that monkeys can't perch there, like the BART station ledges and shop fronts in Berkeley, which have metal spikes to prevent pigeons and the homeless from sleeping there.

The metal rails.

The shards of glass.

When we listen, our past is littered with elegy.

THOUSANDS OF YEARS AGO, Thataka's heart exploded in the forest. Moments before that, she had been soaring towards the sage Vishwamitra and his pupils, Rama and Lakshmana; Ravana had sent her to prevent the sage from performing his yaga. The ritual lasted seven days, but the sage had been prepared—he had brought the two princes to the forest to keep his yaga safe. Pleased, the sage taught Rama mantras to call the spirits to his side. They would turn his arrows into fire. Days later, the three of them approached a lovely grove. The sage chose a place for the fire, sat down, and began another yaga while the two brothers stood on guard like the lids of eyes. It wasn't until the sixth day that a cloud of arms and hammers darkened the sky.

The dark cloud rained flesh towards the fire. Taking aim, Rama pulled his bowstring back and made a roof of arrows in the sky. The earth was covered with the severed heads of rakshasas whose decapitated bodies continued to move, their arms reaching out for direction. Survivors fled beyond the crashing waves of the ocean, where the crystal palaces of the city designed by Maya, the architect of the asuras, welcomed them home.

Pulling out his last arrow, Rama looked at the sun and prayed. This was the first time he pierced Maricha's flesh, not knowing there would be a second, years later.

FROM THE ROOF of Pedda Attha's, you can see the old bus station. There are no signs or markings other than the bustle of people and a stone circle where a man stands, directing traffic. I record the scene for a couple of minutes, right after the singers with cymbals in their hands and skeins of colored fabrics behind them pass by. Then I point the camera towards town. Behind the gopuram of the temple is Jayjayya's house—where Nayanamma used to sleep, where my father collected stamps.

MY FATHER OWNS a small farm on the outskirts of Podili with his cousins. We went there once to see the well they were constructing, a large pit in the earth twenty-five feet across and about that deep, with steps leading along its edges down into darkness. The land used to be dry, but now there are mango trees, coconut trees, green citrus, and rice.

The pujaris join in the chanting. Their different voices synchronize in a circle around the navagrahas as I stand over them, hurling red, white, and yellow petals; Chandra insists that I distribute my offerings evenly. Other pujaris, his seniors, show him his mistakes with a glance and raise their voices above the rest so he can hear the way they know it should be sung. Some of them, like the one to my right, looks at the camera often. They have come from other rituals, ten of the four hundred pujaris who work in town, breaking the stillness of the air with their music, measuring the passing seconds with their cadence.

I find it hard to understand their motives. Did they agree to perform the ritual because of money? I don't deserve their efforts.

Nayanamma would. She bathed snakes with only the sky as protection. She knew what to ask. There are eight pujaris now. One of them who, not noticing the camera, had sat in front of it, slides to the right.

WHEN NAYANAMMA WAS YOUNG, she slept on the floor. The roof was dirt and thatch and parsed with light. When the cobra came, she was dreaming of her future husband, her future son. Her father slept beside her, not dreaming but resting. The cobra watched Nayanamma and then turned to look at him, so he decided to kill it; later, outside, he set it on fire.

You entered my house while we slept; you did not ask. There are no rats here for you, only us. I did what I had to and now your skin is fanned and cracked across the wood. I see my face a thousand times when the sun strikes your skin and then the fire burns them away.

Child, do you know what I whispered into your ear while you slept? If you remember, your life will be what it was meant to be. If you forget, your life will be lost, like many I have chosen not to forgive. I know this like you now know the dead shell of my body beside your feet.

Father, do you know what you have done? If you did, you would have only pushed him away, not killed him, who had done me no harm. What dreams you killed, what a life of debt I have. I nurture the mothers of snakes with milk and honey, I pour them into the holes that are their homes in the morning, take a cold shower with my sari on when the sun rises. And when my children live, I'll make a cobra's eye out of silver and give it to them.

NAYANAMMA, WHEN YOU GAVE BIRTH to your daughter, my Jhansi Attha, you were reborn yourself, your third child pushed your thoughts further apart. Your husband took you to the hospital, where you lived for seven years. You wrote instability into each one of us.

Through cracks in your veins.

The electricity of your voice.

The dried salt under your eyes.

You died not by taking your own life but by an accident, the misfortunate choice of where you decided to put your foot, bare, on a nail. The stars many of us have, like the one on my mother's arm, is the mark of a polio, tetanus, or smallpox vaccination. If you had had one, the tetanus bacteria wouldn't have grown in your foot, sending

poison to your jaw, spreading down to your nerves and spine. Your body, like stiff wood, convulsed, broke.

Do I know my son, my daughter? What do I know but the hands of these doctors? My family can't speak about the filth on the walls of the hospital. From my cot on the roof I stare at the stars. The monkeys have come to crouch. He is with her or he is here. It is so hot, the mosquitoes hum outside the net's wall, the house shakes when the last truck passes by.

I am walking through the long hall of my home. My son is at school, my daughter has grown seven years without me. When I leave, this hall will be filled with pesticides and seeds, bags of fertilizer for the farmers, my husband's customers with white cloth around their hair and their loins, their hands and arms wiry from working the earth. He is with his mistress, and the hall, with its blue walls that will be covered with dust and years of dirt, ends at the well. I will haul up today's water like yesterday and tomorrow.

JAYJAYYA OWNED a small farm on the outskirts of town when my father was young. When I visit, Pedda Attha is afraid that I will get lost. My father had lost his way to the farm as a child, and she thinks I'm as bookish as him. I don't think I could get lost here. There is only one main road. People tell me that Jayjayya showed up one day in Podili and set up a bidi stall. When his father died, his eldest brother, Subbarayadu, inherited the house in Markapur and kicked the rest of the brothers out.

I want to see the well of my grandfather's family in Gajjelakonda, but Pedda Attha tells me it no longer exists. I would find people who never knew our history and a small, dry river near a few thatched roofs.

I fell in a well once, not a very deep one, outside our apartment high-rise in Hyderabad. My fear raised the circle of sky outside higher. It made night cover the walls. I imagined what would happen if I grew tired of paddling. Shadows would march towards the center, tightening their noose around the sun, leaving me to sink in the dark. To raise myself out of the water, I grabbed onto the layers of flat stones jutting from the wall, felt spider webs attach to my wet fingers.

JAYJAYYA'S STALL carried more products over the years, from bidis to mita-paan to cigarettes to pots and pans. He adopted his two nephews and took care of his sister-in-law, Guramma, when his youngest brother died. Jayjayya never spoke to Subbarayudu after what happened in Markapur.

In 1992, he couldn't talk. Sounds from the road surrounded his body made still by age in the old cot at the top of the stairs. His legs and arms were like figs that had fallen from their branches weeks before.

Your eyes reflect what you can't express by holding my hand. The bell rings in the temple you built behind your house that you will fall asleep in, waking up in a place where my hand is gone.

I am here by the well at your house, grandfather. I see a flicker in the dark when I pull water up by the rope. I can't see it, but I hear the sounds of things falling in. Light falls in and returns as shadows. A centipede dances by my feet and I let it, stepping back.

ONCE, I VISITED Jayjayya's other brother, Pitchayya, at his house in Markapur. A heart attack had made him silent; he was lying on a twine and wood cot half in the shade of the front porch of his house. He used to give us colored chalk and slate boards with wood frames from his small factory, and his daughter, only a few years older than us, would string orange flowers in my sister's hair.

Two years later, I would get a telegram. You died in your sleep with a smile on your face.

This time, when I visit, your son takes me from your old wood cot, which no one will sit on, over to your nephew's, and says: *See our cousins across the street? The rest of the family ignores them because of what their father did years ago. But the price they paid was more than our silence. His only son was born unable to speak. He spent sixty years of his life ringing the bell at school. That is all he can do.*

You didn't talk to your nephew, but you watched him grow like a slow tree. Your vows, now burned with your body, no longer keep me from crossing the street.

After so many years of running past their house to play on the hand-cranked Ferris wheel on its summer tour through towns like this one, where everyone was afraid that the wheel would break, spilling us onto the dirt, I met Subbarayudu's only son, my uncle. When I looked into his eyes, he didn't see what we shared. He died on his wood cot and sounds faded around him.

Of chalk on slate.

The ring of a bell.

Lids falling on eyes.

MY FATHER'S MOTHER DIED before I was born. Nayanamma refers to the mother of your father and also to my mother's grandmother on the paternal side. This doubling conflates two people in my mind who differ, and it is hard to keep them apart, to maintain their distinction. My nayanamma, not my mother's, I never met. She, like the other, exists in pictures, now on my parents' kitchen wall. Looking at them you can see they have colored her cheeks rose, and behind her they have added a glow, an aura.

WHEN NAYANAMMA WAS YOUNG, she married my grandfather. Her eldest daughter remembers her today; she turns in front of her altar in the corner of the bedroom because her mother died in August years ago. There is a steel pitcher she anoints with pasupu and kum kum that is as round as Nayanamma's face, as round as the widest part of her arms. I watch the TV fire shots in the air as she rings the bell, circles the air with incense. Pedda Attha is as tall as the small fridge by her bed. *Because of a snake's spirit,* she says, *Nayanamma's children died young, just like the young snake her father had killed.* After two boys and two girls had died, she asked everyone in town, *Why do my children die?* Everyone she asked said that she had a naga dosham. So she went to the new part of town, where there was a huge snake hill with snakes as long as a man's arm. Every day she poured milk and honey on the hill, and then my aunt was born, and then my father, and both were small and frail but lived. She named them after Subrahmanya Swami, because they were his blessings to her. Until she died, she would pray to him by offering milk and honey to the cobras in the hill.

This is a town of pilgrims and sages. One of the pujaris, who sits next to Chandra by the door, speaks Telugu. Chandra turns to him to translate. He looks at me and says, *You have a sarpa dosham, so when you offer flowers, ask for forgiveness from the snake you killed. Pray to her. Ask for what you want. If you know your kuladevatha, pray to her too. She is upset because you have ignored her. When you finish here and return home, perform a puja at your kuladevatha's temple.* I will find out later that a kuladevatha is a local goddess specific to your ancestral home. I will think it is Podilamma, but Pedda Attha will tell me ours is in a temple built by Jayjayya on a hill above Podili. Our family is the only one that prays there. The next time I return, I will walk up that hill.

One ritual leads to others as you progress through the deaths of your family and end up at your own. They hand me the harathi and ask me to turn it around the navagrahas, then bless the small fire burning in ghee three times. I show devotion through rotations; the proof, which is the smoke suspended in the air between this world and another, disappears. I had expected to perform a ritual for the first time without my parents only after my father died. Only sons and brothers are allowed to observe and participate. After a cremation, the bits of bone that survive the fire, called flowers, are collected and scattered in the river. They ask me to pray. I close my eyes.

MY MOTHER SAYS she wants to move into a house that follows vaastu shastra. *It's like feng shui,* she tells me. Vaastu is derived from the Sanskrit word for "house" or "shelter," while "shastra" means "system." Of the five main points one should adhere to, our house violates four of them—houses should not be shaped like ours in an L, there should be no bodies of water in the north or south, ours being situated between Lake Herman and the Carquinez Straits, irregularly shaped plots are forbidden, and the open space around the house should be to the north and the east. What will happen if we don't live in a place according to all these rules? *All of our troubles are tied to this house,* she says. *We have to move.*

 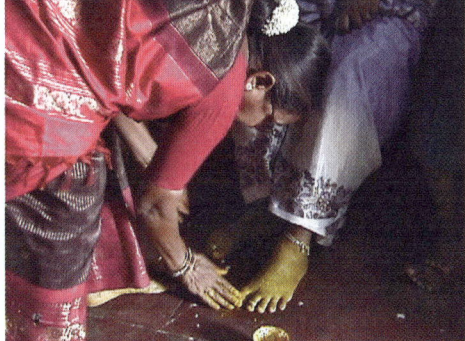 

BEFORE THEY DECIDE on the house, Sharma spends hours in meditation concentrating on a picture my mother has sent. He approves. The house has been built according to vaastu, even if accidentally. The housing plan fits most of the rules, and the few instances where it violates them are easily fixed. My father has the kitchen remodeled so my mother can cook facing east, then adds a second fence along the back of the property so the lot will be a perfect square. He strings fishing wire to create a trellis between the two garages so the house won't have any extensions; it is transformed into a perfect rectangle.

When I see the second fence from the second floor, I think my mother has lost her mind and my father is catering to her whims out of desperation. Years from now, will there be doors that open up to nothing and stairs that lead nowhere?

Maybe these adjustments do nothing to improve the flow of energy through the house or prevent a spirit from residing there. But they improve my mother's spirit, because in her psyche, in her narrative of herself, listening to her seer is the right thing to do. It is what her mother, and her mother's mother, have always done.

THE DAY PEDDA ATTHA has all the women, including her Muslim neighbors, over for a ceremony, we watch her go through the motions. She rubs pasupu on their legs. I track her hands with my video camera. I hope they will talk about the lives they lead on this street, where I have seen them from the balcony as they pump water in groups of two, helping each other prepare for the day. Balancing silver jugs of water on their hips, they carry them back and forth to houses roofed with shingles or colorful concrete or nothing more than a layer of palm leaves. Thirst has held them together for this long.

But instead of telling their stories to me, they are fascinated by my friend Chris; they have never met someone with skin as white as his. The young women giggle and ply him with questions, nod blankly when he says he is a writer.

After they leave, Pedda Attha's daughter, Ramasubbulu, notices that one of the young women has sat down with a sodi across the street. She goes over and takes her turn as I watch. I am too confused to switch on the camera, even though she gestures for me to do so.

RAMASUBBULU TELLS ME that Pitchayya, our grand-uncle, loves and misses her. His spirit is one of the ones the sodi has seen, and the sodi asks Ramasubbulu to appease him by offering a pancha. She wipes a tear above her smile and says, *Why should I do that? Pitchayya has his own sons and daughters to do that for him! Why didn't you videotape that? Even people here rarely see a sodi.*

Luckily, the downstairs neighbor, Jaya, also wants to have her gadde, or story, told. She asks Ramasubbulu and Pedda Attha to help; it's her first gadde. I turn the video camera on and look through the viewfinder. Her two kids run around the muggu painted on the awning of the doorway until the sodi comes over and sits down, propping her gourd coated with years of pasupu against the wall. Focusing on her from the stairs above, each thread of silk in her sari is saturated with color. Each ridge under her eyes bears practice.

Jaya asks the sodi, *Will you tell me my gadde for 5 rupees?*

You can't bargain for your gadde. Five quarts of grain only costs 10 rupees. Just one word of your gadde is worth it. Anyone can ask questions, but I am the one who can mediate between you and the spirits. You have to follow traditions. It's not my story, but your story that I will tell.

From behind us on the steps, Pedda Attha says, *You should not listen to someone else's story.*

NAYANAMMA, DID YOU FEAR *the unexplained diseases that robbed you of your children, the sixteen who found their escape in an early death? You married into this task barely older than your children who died so young. Your husband, returning home from the open hillsides of slate, having mined it for his wealth, having built his riches out of the black rock, did he only have one wish of you? To have a child? And when he achieved that was your task done, holding onto the wall, aged with black eyes and the white strands of hair you had left?*

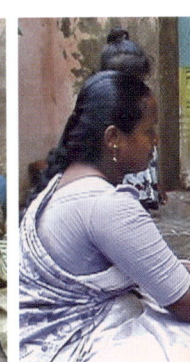

AFTER RAMA KILLED RAUANA, he returned with his wife Sitha to Rameswaram. To expiate the sin of killing, he performed a puja for Shiva. He sent Hanuman to fetch a lingam from Kashi, but he was delayed. The moment for the ceremony was close at hand. Leaning down to the earth, Sitha made a lingam out of sand, and the two of them performed the ceremony. When Hanuman arrived, he tried to destroy the sand lingam, but it was impervious to his efforts. Rama, seeing this, said to him: *Hanuman, from now on, there will be two lingams here at Rameswaram. Your lingam will be worshipped, and the mud lingam will also be worshipped, but never before yours.*

THE SODI PRAYS to gods I have never heard of before, the ones in trees and in rocks, the ones deep inside the mounds of snakes. The tamboura dictates her tempo as she sings to Jaya, *Show me your hand. I will tell you your story.* She speaks in gestures and teaches us what her movements mean. If the spirit is male, *I touch your chin. If it is female, I touch your bottu. If it's from the family that gave birth to you, it's asking for food. If it's from the one you bought, I touch your stomach.* With Jaya's hand, she makes a dizzying blur; I see her touch Jaya's chin and her bottu. She describes dying traditions with idioms and phrases long out of daily use, like her profession, which she is one of the last to practice.

The spirit says to Jaya, *For four years, I entangled your body in fever and confusion. Day by day, you lost hope. You cursed in pain. You ask why. I will tell you. I lost myself; my maya overcame me. I had come to bless you. Now, I come to remind you.*

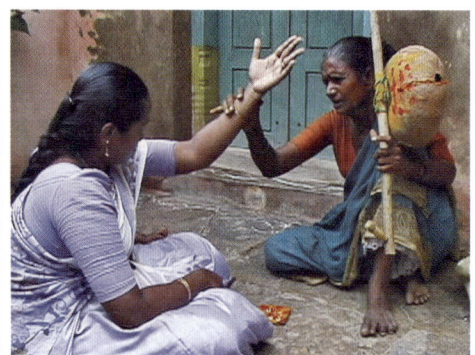

Ramasubbulu yells at the spirit, *You should ask for what you need! Why are you making her suffer?*

You won't do what I want unless you feel what I do. You try to heal. You take medicine, but I turn it into sewage. I can't stop myself. No one else can control you with their maya.

Jaya and Ramasubbulu ask in unison, *Why did you come?*

I was discontent.

Which side did you come from?

I am from this side. She waves to her right at the wall above her head where pink paint is flaking off from the sun's heat, revealing an older shade below.

Are you a close relative or a distant one?

I am the distant past life of a relative. I can make you feel like you are drinking water from the Ganges. In my life, none of my wishes were met. I want to give you the joy of meeting your own. But as long as I am lost in your body, I can only create pain.

Ramasubbulu stands up and tells Jaya, *Take her over to your in-law's house. They will take care of it. Isn't there a good person there?*

I think to myself, is this another Sharma, like my mother's?

She can ask the spirit what needs to be done, Ramasubbulu says to her mother, then asks the sodi, *What should I do?*

The sodi rises to adjust her faded green sari and says, *Get a yanthram tied.*

Jaya and Ramasubbulu quip, *Yanthram-tanthram!*

Tie it while burning incense. If you light it on fire, it will burn like a person on their funeral pyre. With one harsh blow, the spirit will never come back. No chance in a lifetime for her!

The sodi then turns to me, laughs, and says, *Ask for your gadde in Hyderabad. One man comes around there.* In a city of more than ten million, I think, one man would be hard to find.

I keep my eyes closed. Around me, they are waiting, cross-legged before the blue wall, or next to Chandra in front of the pink one. Where the two colors meet in the corner of the room, there is nothing but empty space. They ask me to pray, but I have nothing left to ask.

I wait for my memories to finish jogging. For a decade, the India I knew never changed. Under the balance in the cabinet of his shop, Jayjayya still kept three silver coins from the turn of the century for luck. When he looked out into the street, my India was there to greet him.

The balcony at the top of the stairs is no longer there. The floor has fallen off into the air above the road. A few metal rods, once held in concrete, dangle where a wall used to be. Across the street, the neighbor is staring out of what once was the front of his house. All our balconies have disappeared, leaving us open to the road below.

WHEN WE ARE ABOUT TO LEAVE for the station, Pedda Attha sees someone walk in front of the house and tells me to wait. "Why?" I ask. She says it is bad luck to cross paths with someone from a lower caste at the beginning of a long journey.

The day before, she had performed a Hindu ceremony, inviting her Muslim neighbors over and covering their feet in pasupu. Today, she is following narrow, caste-based superstitions.

I board the bus, which smells of a hundred bodies, all destined to sweat from a million pores into one metal box headed east, towards the ocean, towards Ongole, where Jhansi Attha lives. The woman sitting in front of me asks what I am doing and where I am from. Her next set of questions, after finding out I am from the U.S., are predictable: *What's your job, how much do you make, are you a citizen?* The question that follows is one I didn't expect. *What is your caste?* Why do you ask? *Oh, we don't pay attention to it.* If you didn't pay attention to it, you wouldn't ask. *What's your name then?* Amar. *No, your surname.* It's Ravva. *You're a vaishya then.* She is smug.

THE HOUSE IS OFF THE MAIN ROAD in Ongole and is long and narrow like the inside of a Victorian row house, though the outside is angular and rough cement; in the old commercial district, every house is enclosed on all sides by other houses like this one. Jhansi Attha rents out the top two floors and lives on the first, which has no windows. In front is a shop that faces the street. About eight feet wide by ten feet deep, it has plenty of sunlight and contains a desk and small chair, around which are rows of modular shelving that house a variety of neatly stacked colored paper. Her husband has a lucrative business selling government forms for every legal, civic, and property-related transaction in town as well as in the county, since Ongole is the seat of the Prakasam district.

Jhansi Attha spends afternoons in the shop; her husband is often away on trips with the Rotary Club. She enjoys grabbing my cheeks with her hard grip and bops me on the head to show affection. She is loud and crass. I flinch and feel at home. On the road, a pack of barking wild dogs passes by. A male and female are locked together, while the rest circle around trying to disengage them. Blood drips down their legs.

After the barking moves down the street, she tells me that Jayjayya took her out of school pretty early, before what they call intermediate in India and what we in the U.S. would call high school. He thought she didn't need to learn anymore. *All of the things I do here in the shop, I learned on my own.*

When she was young, people remembered her with her father in his shop. Her large eyes, like her mother's, he kept close. Her sharp tongue, like her mother's, made him laugh. She followed his example. What she learned from her father never failed her.

97

EVERYONE IN ANDHRA has a dosham. Many children are named after Subrahmanya Swami, only the reasons why differ, says my father. Like him, both of his cousins are named Subbarao, and so are two of mine. Two of the pujaris have "subba" in their names as well. Do they all have a dosham? My father would find it hard to believe that they did. On most days, he would categorize all this as superstition, or maybe the result of a collective rationale that orders and transforms what can't be understood into something that has a name.

To my mother, my father is like a rock kept dry by an unknown set of circumstances in the middle of a river rushing downstream. When she needs it, she makes use of the stable foothold he offers.

WHEN JAYJAYYA'S ELDER BROTHER DIED, my great aunt's eyes were bright green. Years later, they have grown darker. Guramma makes me okra and fried bitter gourd, a favorite dish on my father's side of the family, and doesn't cry like she usually does when I visit her. Instead, she tells me a story about being a farmer's daughter in a small village called Mani Vamilu.

My mother's mother couldn't have children. She gave birth to two cobras, and her family raised them on milk and fruit for more than a hundred years. Her family had leased their rice fields to a farmer and would split the harvest with him. He traded his sweat for their land. Their children, the cobras, left the hut each morning and measured the grain, cleaving them into equal piles by sliding through the sand.

One day, a wedding took place in the house. During the ceremony, we gave huge offerings of pongali in large brass containers, sarava, to god. While we made the pongali, the snakes didn't go anywhere. They were curled up asleep, one next to the other.

At night, it was dark; there was no current in those days. The cooks took a sarava and put it on top of the cobras by accident. When everyone realized what had happened, they prayed to Govinda, hoping to call him into the house. Usually, before a meal, they would feed the snakes. This time, they offered food and prayed to chinna nagamayya and pedda nagamayya—but they didn't come, because they had died.

For a wedding dinner, it became too quiet, and the neighbors wondered why. When they opened the door, everyone was sitting in front of their plates made of bo leaves, but they had no mouths and no eyes.

The next morning, everyone fasted and took coconuts, flowers, balls of sesame, rice, and jaggery to the snake mound. They poured some milk, and their eyes and mouths reappeared. From then on, they fasted on that day every year. That is why cobras were born in that house.

Mani Vamilu is not far from Podili, where Guramma tells me this story in a small house with fading bluish green walls, a stack of papers behind her head. This town is no different. Full of farmers who remember the past, stacking these stories like stones. With them they make four walls, and when they are done, they go inside, call it home.

AT JHANSI ATTHA'S, I GET ILL and spend a week in pools of cold sweat from chills, though it's the dead of summer, when the heat melts sandals to the road. To my right is a dresser; to my left, a huge safe that has been around my grandfather most of his life. When Jhansi Attha was married, Jayjayya gave them to her from his house in Podili. As I slip in and out of consciousness, I have a vision of a tunnel with a shining light at its end. I walk towards it. The tunnel becomes a rooftop, and Jayjayya is looking at me like he used to, his eyes a little wet. I wake up and stare at the mother of pearl in the doors of the dresser, then the blackened rust in the grooves of the safe.

When I recover, I videotape the objects unique to our family's history—the dresser and the safe and Jhansi Attha's collection of family photos. I take stills of them in the brightest part of the house, the puja room. Under a fluorescent tube, framed pictures of deities line all four walls up to the top of the high ceiling. Their eyes, surrounded by gold and flowers, stare down at me.

JHANSI ATTHA'S HUSBAND smokes a cigarette on the platform in Ongole. Orange embers extinguish themselves around his feet. I check the clock. The train is late. Hundreds of flies scatter off a burlap sack as a man wipes his sweat. Have I missed it already? I can't see any English signs up and down the length of the one that has just pulled in; in this town, they only stop for a moment. Before I can figure out where it is going, it glides away. I beg my uncle to check with the station agent to see if mine has already passed through. A few seconds later, as another one pulls in, I run to the station agent's kiosk and yell, "Is it this one?" Behind me, a monkey skitters by and I glimpse its long, thin tail. We are far from the platform and even further away from where my cabin should come to a halt. We race to the closest AC car and my uncle throws me on, luggage and all. I look up at an agent, who is scowling in the doorway to the compartment. Instead of coming to a stop, the train has begun to pick up speed. There will be no bustle of luggage or bodies through these doors. I am on the wrong train, going anywhere, with the wrong ticket.

When India stirred, the British left. Slipped into the seams of jackets, under the cover of mass migrations and cities set aflame, pieces of India left with them. In the wake of separation, under the flow of bodies exchanging one country for another, the colonial railways rusted. In England, they must have regretted this loss. But what they took in exchange, the Koh-i-Noor diamond, is now the jewel of the crown.

In the 1800s, the East India Company built a steam engine and track to transport commodities a distance of twenty-one miles. Two hundred years later, there are 65,000 kilometers of railway, two million employees, and one lost traveller in the middle of this mercantile masterwork. The agent demands to see my ticket. He knows I have the wrong one. Five times the cost of my ticket in bribes and payoffs manage to correct

102

my mistake, and when I finally switch to the right train in Vizag, a porter is determined not to leave me alone until he takes the rest of my money.

An hour into my refusing the porter's demands, an incredibly drunk man in the bunk across from mine wakes up and yells at him. *Come here! I'll give you what you want!* Relieved, I lock up my belongings with the chain I carry around with me. In the heart of this metal beast, I have found my place. The train moves through the night, dropping a stream of feces from its bathrooms. After it passes, people squat on the tracks, making their own contributions.

THIN STRIPS OF EARTH border the backwaters, dotted with lights at night and kids flying kites during the day. Behind them stretch water, wood poles, and lilies. We rent a house boat and eat fish caught at dawn. The fisherman's song carries for miles in the morning. They sing to each other of water and fish in canoes black with sap. They pierce the air like radio waves, and their nets of twisted fiber, made by sinewy hands, break the reflected sky.

When my cell phone rings, I am videotaping a kingfisher perched on an electrical wire. Even out in Kerala's backwaters, cell phones work. India adopted cellular technology much later than other countries, so its infrastructure is far better than what I experience in the U.S. On the other end of the line is Ganesh. The last time we spoke, he told me twenty-four people were gathering at his place; he was disappointed I couldn't come to do interviews. He said I should be careful about what I ate. This time, he asks if I will come to Lucknow before I leave.

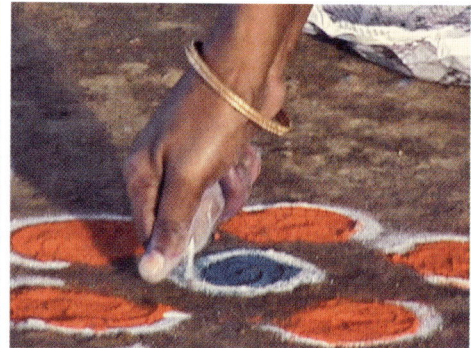

WHY DO YOU WALK *the entire length of India from Rishikesh to Rameswaram?* I once asked Ganesh.

Have you ever wondered what jet lag is? It is not caused by changing time zones or your circadian rhythms being off. It is fatigue from having the atoms of your body move so fast through the air. That is why I walk. In Rameswaram, an interesting thing happened that has never happened before in our history. Vishnu prayed to Shiva. Gods had never prayed to each other before.

I DRIVE UP to my parent's house in American Canyon and notice that my mother has carefully written "OM" in Sanskrit on both of the garage doors. Preoccupied by memories of the apartment in Berkeley I have just moved out of, I don't ask her about it. For years, I looked out onto a world of sororities and fraternities. I could never figure out why the busses that took the students to their social events had to run idle for hours while the girls primped their hair and got ready for their group dates with their fraternity brothers. Or why their parents would park their Astrovans on the street—a place half as wide as the cul de sac I imagine they had driven from—blocking traffic for hours. I'm not sure why my mother's blessing on her garage doors in our suburban tract home development makes me uncomfortable. Perhaps my impulse is to hide what makes us different.

Inside, I overhear CNN on the television. The news is saturated with terror alerts, dirty bombs, anthrax. Colin Powell points at several canisters in the desert. I wonder how many people are lying awake in their beds waiting for the next plane crash, the suitcase that will explode, or the letter in the mail that will infect. If they dream of airports with armed guards.

In other countries, the guards go unnoticed because they have been there for so long. People dream of starvation.

Burning sand. Children in the ruins of tanks. Skylines.

-- : -- : -- : --

At the beginning of a tape, the lights around us—*the visible*—have yet to leave their impression. We lock away what we are sure to forget.

A year before I performed the naga prathista in Rameswaram, all my DV tapes plus the hard drive with my edits were lost. Someone had stolen the backpack they were in, leaving only the fading images in my memory—screaming dogs, a singing monkey, my cousin's face as he watched the camera. The digitized transmission of history from aunt to nephew, grandmother to grandson, mother to son, no longer exists.

It took me ten years to return to India, after earning enough money for a ticket, the camera, and twenty hours of tape.

I imagine the drive has been erased, leaving no trace of the stories my family told to explain who we are. Its new owners, faced with a void like the myth of the pioneer's empty West, will do what they must— they will populate it; they will construct an archive of their own.

Erasing a drive only destroys the surface index, not the binary code that marks the instances of magnetic repulsion and attraction that lie beneath. Behind the veil of its emptiness, a small town in India still remains.

The past is written over with new ones and zeros. An entry in the index is created so they can be found again. This new data is stored randomly, and all around it are dispossessed strings of numbers that have no entry, have no name to be called by anymore. When I had stored them, they were light and shade on a dirt road, or the colors of buildings baked by heat.

By now, most of those strings will be gone. They have been replaced by the traces of someone I will never know, who bought them for a price that will always be too low.

The few that are left are small—part of a face, a sliver of sky, a woman's laugh. If we could ever see them, they would haunt us like the fragments of ancient poems that can never be fully reconstructed. A word, perhaps two, fills us with horror; we turn away from a tear in the fabric. We imagine the rest of the poem. We dream of the sky that is missing.

THE WINTER MY SISTER CALLED to tell me what happened, I thought of your hair. In my notebooks, Radhika, I drew your ribbons in orange surrounded by black hair, knowing you were upset by suitors who refused you.

My mother and father have left for business. The day grows frightful. Am I ugly, unlovable? Why does no one want me? No one will. I'm in the blue hall with these pesticides, with this rat poison. This one is my groom, my love.

AFTER THE FIRST MONSOON RAIN, Ganesh stops drinking water. This time, unlike before, he suffers from kidney failure. Mr. Nagi is unable to take care of him, so Ganesh leaves Rishikesh to stay with his mother in Lucknow. I realize now that the first time I called, she was the woman who had answered. For her, Ganesh never renounced the material world, which included her and the rest of his family. He was still her Raj Kumar. How upset was she when he returned with the uncut facial hair of a sadhu, wrapped in an orange loincloth, suffering from kidney failure?

When Ganesh first told me that he survived on a glass of milk each day and existed only on air during the monsoon, I found it hard to believe him. It defied logic. How could he survive? Through research, I discovered that yogis were known to practice extreme forms of physical denial; some, who abstained from food and water, claimed to live off of only prana, or sustenance through light. Like many stories of the past, I expect these to be exaggerations. But after Ganesh's kidneys fail, I begin to question my doubts. This is logical. A person who gives up drinking water would suffer from kidney failure.

WHEN GANESH ASKED ME to follow him around with a video camera so he could prove to the rest of the world that he didn't drink water or eat food, I knew there would always be gaps; batteries die, the tape ends, machines break. From the blank spaces, the moments lost in the record, doubts would rise in the minds of the people he was trying to convince. Completely automated surveillance systems, like those used in malls, are able to provide a complete record of what is being watched. With a portable version of such a system, I could conceivably follow him. But who would watch me to ensure that I never averted my gaze, letting Ganesh sneak some food? Another person would have to videotape me as I documented Ganesh. And then another person would have to watch that person, and so on, until all of us were caught in the circular ruins of our eyes.

BEHIND EVERY FIRE is something greater. We imagine a center. It has flames that illuminate every direction and a myriad of spokes that radiate outwards to form a circle with an infinite number of points. If the center were to consume all around it, like Shiva in his cosmic dance at the end of existence, or if it were to remain dormant, like the universe before the Big Bang, it would be the only point in the middle of nothingness. The ancient Brahmin seers speculated that it was stationary and beyond space, time, and causation. The rest of us they called jivatmas. We revolve. Undergo birth and death because we are bound. We hurtle through space and measure each second. Centrifugal force, called maya, pulls us towards the periphery.

atma

---

spirit

HISTORY IS UNEARTHED in Southampton, California. Vents of methane gas jet out of cracks in the dirt beneath the tract homes that stretch from the straits up past our house to Lake Herman. Along Rose Drive, the air clings to swing sets like the spindly whites of old eggs. The earth opens up and swallows entire backyards. Foundations we never had cause to question are now cleaved and splintered. My friend, who has grown up in an old Victorian down by the waterfront, laughs and says, *We all knew that there was a landfill. I dumped stuff there with my dad once or twice. The developers covered it up with dirt and built on top of it.*

INSIDE OUR HOMES there was no need to look beyond the milky counter top and the newly installed beige carpet. It softened to our touch. When you do look at what forms the strata beneath, you may be able to find a record of three hundred years. In those layers lie cholera and smallpox. Tule thatch and acorn. Upon the rolling hills towards Lake Herman, war broke out between the Spaniards and the *People of the West Wind*. The Spaniards pushed them back to where the city of Suisun is today. They retreated to the rush huts of their village. Enclosed by willow saplings and the tall marsh grasses they used to create their homes, families chose to die rather than become slaves to the missionaries. They lit their walls on fire and let themselves be carried by the wind. Their ceremonial song, sung at the moment of death, rose into the air.

AT NIGHT, we follow the Feather River from Reno among controlled forest fires. They flicker in the snow on either side of us as we drive to a pink trailer up the road from The Express Coffee Shop in Quincy. After warming up with beer and quesadillas, my friend Dave asks if we want to go on a walk. It is midnight and there is no moon to illuminate the mountain tree lines. The road behind the school stretches up into the darkness; he wants us to walk up the hill, one by one, 50 feet apart, and meet him at the top. We lose sight of each other in the dark, looking at shadows of gray on shades of black. Twenty minutes later, I see him leaning against the shell of an abandoned VW Bug at the top of the hill.

He asks, *Did you see anything?* and I say, *I saw shapes in the trees.*

One by one he asks each of us as we arrive at the top. After we are all there, he says, *This is Cemetery Hill, where the Chinese who worked on the transcontinental railroad were buried.* The imprint of what he tells me takes the "shapes" and assigns them a narrative, forms them into the people who once worked here.

At Promontory Point in 1869, Leland Stanford drove a spike of Californian gold into the earth and joined thousands of miles of Union Pacific track with seven hundred miles of Central Pacific track. In the photograph of the "driving of the Golden Spike," none of the Chinese immigrants are visible, even though they had graded the site hours before. More than a century later, an Asian American documentary filmmaker will superimpose her ancestors onto the spaces they would have occupied next to the other railroad workers. Their ghosts have finally found embodiment in our history.

I TELL MY MOTHER, *They used to live here.* They left mounds of discarded shells along the shores of the straits that were ground up under waterfront developments made of sails and yachts, styrofoam swordfish, brick walkways, white paint. Their dead, wrapped in bear hide, were buried under these homes. They wound them round and round with rope. They dug with sticks. When a bird stopped at the lake's edge, they shot it and ate it with fish. But, I tell her, all of this could also have been made up—the figment of an anthropologist's imagination. Beneath our carpet, under the grey cement foundation, beneath a layer of trash, under thousands of years of historical conjecture, could be the bones of a Patwin. They were southern Wintun, neighbors with the Maidu.

THE FIRST SPANISH EXPLORER to the valley saw a river full of feathers. It led south down to plains full of antelope and grizzly bear where the maidum, or the people of the valley, died one summer. They lay fevered under shade trees near water while the skulls of others lay beside them.

In 1830, a sailor returning from the Pacific and another man, a trapper named John Work, carried fever and ague to the Central Valley, where it killed three-quarters of California's indigenous people. European settlers had evolved with what anopheles had bred and carried in bogs and the dead, still pools of the old world, but the genes of the Americas had had no time to adapt to what the dark ages of Europe had called the stench of swamps, *mala aria* or "bad air." Unsickled blood flowed through bodies worn thin under the collars of the Spanish, the little they had to eat chipped away at by winter and spring's debt.

COYOTE MAN SAYS back then the people of the Valley and the people of the South always fought. Lured by the promise of peace, the South People went to the Valley People's roundhouse at Sucker Run for a big feast. The story goes that once the South People were inside, the Valley People set it on fire.

The South People had great doctors. They called forth a poison air that went here and there, killing all of the people in the valley.

A DECADE LATER, Peter Lassen would follow the Pit River to Big Meadow, where the Maidu always shared their salmon with newcomers. A doctor in the roundhouse sang that change would come like the wild turkeys and hogs that bred in the foothills.

Why are you here? What will you see when you open your eyes? Madhwa Brahmins say we are no more than specks of dust that must do what we can for each other out of compassion. How can we expect to be heard by something infinite amidst all our suffering? I agree. When we come together in ceremony, we share what ails us.

I have been entranced by the hum of voices. When the pujaris were young, they were taught to sing Sanskrit for hours as they are doing now; as young men, they learned austerity at our back doors while asking for food. When their father tied the knot of the thread around their chest, they were born for a second time, celibate until they became pujaris themselves. They tap my shoulder against the blue wall.

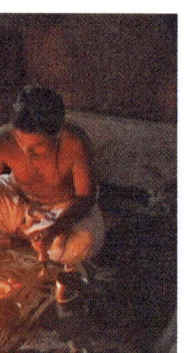

BELOW WHERE TERMINAL GEYSER GASPS, we sit in pools of heat. The steam rises, covers our bodies, our skin soaked with sulfur, our clothes neat on the rocks. Above us, on the hill, yellow mats of bacteria drip hot water and bees circle the patches they make. The four of us are nudes carved from soapstone surrounded by rain.

We shelter our utterances from loss. We had walked from Willow Lake Bog, trailed by watercress and scarlet larkspur. In one of our books from that day, a bloom died on a page. In the morning, we had crossed a ridge and entered a clearing in the woods. These lands were empty of people, but in front of us we saw four nests where animals had slept the night before, when we had been caught in the rain, when we had experimented with tarps and gravity. They looked freshly abandoned. Dena said they were deer nests. I imagined the deer asleep, grass piled up around them.

Lake Almanor now glistens where Big Meadow once stretched for miles between the mountains. At its center is the Big Spring that quenched Maidu thirst; nowadays, the spring only gives its water to the empty pits of their flooded burial grounds. *This is where we summered*, Dena tells me. *We buried our dead here. In the meadow, we ate acorn. We had our dance.*

WHEN GOLD WAS FOUND, the miners came to the mountains like sheets of falling sand. Sorties of soldiers from the armory in Benicia followed, cleansing California of its "wild savages." The State paid a total of one million dollars for scalps, ranging from $5 in Shasta to 25 cents at Honey Lake.

The salmon would no longer run in rivers choked with the tailings of mountains and the mercury left behind by the leaching operations of George Hearst and other gold barons. Sediment flowed down to the Central Valley, causing floods in Marysville and raising the floor of San Francisco Bay by three feet.

Chandra hands me a clump of plant stalks—wheat, rice, or hay—and positions them so they connect me with the navagrahas. They arc between my body and the planets. He tells me to concentrate, as if I could will my desires through the stalks into the brass vessels. What does the camera see? My closed eyes and the stalks in my hand? Flower laden steel surrounded by fabrics, bananas, nuts, and the ribbons of rice flower that jet out from beneath? The expression on my face? Is it one of faith? Or is it curiosity? Or obedience?

The pujaris begin chanting again. I try to understand what is being said. What is being hurled into the air around me.

  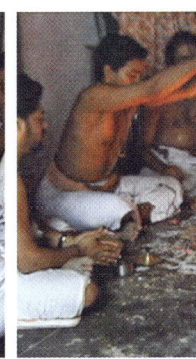

WHEN THE SALMON stopped running, the maidum exchanged their nets and hooks for picks and pans. At outposts, they traded a pound of gold for a pound of beef.

The state envisioned the Indians cordoned off in pockets under watch where they would learn to farm far from the mother lode in the Sierras. The maidum were driven for miles on long walks into the valley where land planted with wheat waited for their efforts. Maidu trails of tears crossed the foothills; the women would sleep in trees, where they were safe from rape by "drunken brawlers who wished at a very unreasonable hour to pay their devours to the sleeping beauties of the train." With time, they would slip away from the reservations of Round Valley or Nome Lackee and return to their only true home in the mountains. Once there, they would find most of their community scattered and without land.

In 1850, before the state became part of the Union, Senator John Bidwell drafted the "Act for the Government and Protection of Indians," allowing him and others to buy and enslave the Maidu like the missionaries had yoked other tribes a century before. Hundreds of maidum panned the Hamilton-Bidwell mining claims, now under Lake Oroville, using wood bowls and baskets. The operation netted Bidwell a mansion; he paid the maidum in "pink rag quarters" they hung on string around their necks.

Under the mountains, the Chinese blasted apart rock, laid rails, and drove spikes until they met the Irish on the other side of Utah doing the same. The east and west coasts were joined by iron hammered into the earth. The door to the west was open, and the east came armed with demands and designs, claims and capital, spouse and spawn. On the other side waited fantasies kept safe by ridges and impasse; the new migrants watched it loom as they rode the railroad into the dark mouth dug inside.

By the 1900s, only half of the Maidu were left. In Big Meadow, some ranched or continued to mine for gold barons, while others held onto their land as change poured in around them. In the center of the roundhouse, the doctor's song would remind them, *These people will crowd us out. We must get out of the way.*

WHEN JULIUS HOWELLS envisioned electricity from a bluff that overlooked Big Meadow, he submerged a church, along with a town, underwater. He cut trees and created towns around its edge. He supplied power to the hungry cities downstream and beyond. In the cities, "white coal" was on their lips; they grasped for Owens Valley, the Hetch Hetchy, the Feather River basin. Land around Prattville and the Maidu was bought by proxy; Great Western Power approached John's son, Augustus, to sway his neighbors in the meadow. Under the pretense of expanding the family ranch, he gathered most of the valley and brought Howells a step closer to his dream.

For the Maidu, who could not forget John Bidwell's deception only a generation before, his son's efforts served only to increase their desire to hold onto their land. GWP brought its first condemnation suit against the Maidu in 1902. The State ruled in the company's favor; electricity was for the "greater good" of its people even though this meant placing a river in the hands of a private company. GWP bought the land immediately, but the issue of title haunted them until long after the dam was built. The Government had never given the Maidu title to their lands in the first place, so the area under the lake did not belong to either party until 1921, when Congress gave the native lands to the company in a special act.

At the other end of the meadow, Prattville waited to become a resort town on the shore of the yet-to-be-born lake. Its residents joined a small group of local settlers and ranch owners who would not sell. Some could not give up their homes, while others imagined better offers for their property as San Francisco's demands for white coal grew.

The entire town was a mile away for a baseball game when a fire torched Prattville to the ground. Those who still owned their land, sold. The remains of a church, an old cemetery, and Maidu burial sites were moved to higher ground in 1914, but as the waters of Lake Almanor rose, all the newly relocated pits were swept away. Beads and money slipped back to their former place of rest as if they had never moved. Along the new shore, they washed into prospecting hands.

Ravi gets up and turns off the video camera. We had agreed to this with the other pujaris, who were allowing me to make a false record— one that was discontinuous and incomplete—of the prathista. Was it so that I wouldn't violate a rule? Or so no one could learn to imitate the intricacies of their ritual?

In Podili, I would record ceremonies and interview Pedda Attha about doshams, or try to videotape the gods in the temples. She would tell me these things weren't meant to be taped, but would help me ask, would try to mediate a compromise. If that didn't work, she would hustle me in anyway. I would videotape until the devotees turned their attention away from god, inciting the wrath of the attending pujari.

Towards the end of the day, the parts of the prathista that take place in the temple also can't be recorded. Cameras and non-Hindus are not allowed inside.

SOMEWHERE NEAR KEDDIE RIDGE is a lake, and at the bottom of this lake is a hole. The young maidum who searched for it were rarely successful. But occasionally, someone wouldn't break through the blue surface with their last breath of air. They had found what they were looking for; they had entered the hole, not knowing where it led.

SOMETIMES THE YOUNG who disappeared in the lake never returned. Other times they would come back just in time for a dance. They would rise out of the river in Big Meadow, even as late as two weeks after they had vanished, to dry by the fire while the rest questioned silently. The maidum at Big Spring were glad when someone chose to come back; it was the only answer they needed.

The maidum say that the journey takes you more than five miles under the mountain. The young maidum who ventures down there begins to dream without the sun; he has passed from our world into another and brought some of that world back with him. In the roundhouse, they make space for their new doctor and wait. His song will rattle in the night.

THE CARIBOU WILDERNESS surrounds my sleeping body stretched out upon the dirt and rock, the flattened pine. The mosquitoes sense my heat, my blood. They breed in the still pools around us. Trickling streams aquify the earth and produce patches of watercress with blue flowers as I slip and run through the swamp, where a small river loads the lake, until I find myself in a patch of trees. One has fallen on the ground, rising about four feet into the air. I sit down. I get up. I walk back and forth on the log, and that is when they notice me. The first pheasant rises up from the forest floor. As quickly as the first, four more rustle away, showing their tail feathers in russet colors.

The lake is sped over by large dragonflies, still and reflecting their humming bodies, the mud moving slightly in the shallow pools. Circled by pollen, we swim to the tree lightning has left standing in the shape of a hand. Beneath us, an old forest is waiting for drought after having been buried under years of snow.

MAIDU MEDICINE MEN who were nearing death would make a final journey to Bald Rock Dome, a massive cliff that rises 2,000 feet above the waters of the middle fork of the Feather River. It is said that they would sit at the edge of a crevice until they lost consciousness and fell peacefully into the river below.

IN GENESEE, I hear the train curving along the valley. The noise had scared the Maidu when they first heard it; it was a sound signaling colonization. My friend Farrell—one of the last and the youngest fluent Yamani or Mountain Maidu speakers—says that when the gold miners came to Indian Valley, they settled in a place called Coppertown. It was there that his ancestors began wearing jeans, took their first sip of alcohol. One of the Maidu, a medicine man named Shim, lived amongst them, but began to resent the changes he witnessed. The roundhouse made way for the wood cabin; the mortar and acorn were replaced by whiskey and tin. They say medicine men can see the dead, and Shim was no different. After the Europeans came, not only did he see the spirits of the dead maidum, but also the dying spirit of the living maidum. Angry, he began to curse everyone who adopted European ways. The maidum knew that he was using his power against them. They could feel him probing in their dreams. Banished from Coppertown, he set up across the river at a place they now call Shim's Flat. From this bend in the river, he could see the town in the distance.

I ask Farrell why they think the flat is haunted. He likes to tell stories, and this one is about one of his ancestors, so he doesn't hesitate to explain. Shim was a medicine man, and it was commonly known that the only way to kill a medicine man was while he was engaged in a ceremony. One night, when Shim was in the roundhouse, chanting and singing in front of the fire and shaking a small rattle called a sokoti, a group of maidum snuck in and axed him. They said it had to be done because Shim was killing the Maidu with his magic, that he had become a hudesi, a person who kills without reason. Farrell's ancestors burned Shim's roundhouse and all of his possessions, but they knew his spirit was still around. They knew he had become a kokini, a ghost.

Ravi walks in front of the camera and sits down amidst a torrent of chanting. The two serpents stand upright on a bed of uncooked reddish-brown rice in a room louder and brighter than before. Chandra holds a necklace made of betel leaves and threads it around the rock. The leaves stick out from behind the snakes like a fan of peacock feathers, shading them. He asks me to tie the knot of the necklace, then sets the serpents on their side. He hands me a large plate and instructs me to bury the serpents in rice by moving his hands across the surface of the stone, from bottom to top. I follow with a stream of rice that falls from the plate's edge. I wipe my nose; it runs, I have a cold.

Like Chris's, my body has succumbed to a germ caught on the train from Rishikesh to Delhi. It is my first summer cold. Watching my friend adjust to the microbes his body can't recognize—it had no genetic history of this place locked away within its cells—reminds me that I have been spared until now because my body still remembers my last visit two summers ago. Most Indians I know get sick when they return to India. Our cells have forgotten their early memories and need reminding.

BEFORE WE CAMP at Shim's Flat, we have dinner at the house of Dena and Farrell's parents. They are smoking at a small table next to the window. The sun has set, and the wood paneling of the house makes the room dim. We tell them we are going to spend the night at Shim's, and they both smile and drag on their cigarettes. Their mother, Joyce, is happy because Farrell is going to take the bear to his place for the year. Ever since the previous year's dance, the bear has lived upstairs in Dena's old bedroom. She says a lot of strange things have happened, that sometimes you can hear the bear talk, or he injects thoughts into your head. Lily, who spent a couple of nights sleeping in the room, had had a hard time because the bear had been too noisy and had kept her up. I look at them a little incredulously and repeat, *Strange things?* Dena's dad, Marvin, turns away from the window to look at us when he says, *Sure, there's all sorts of strange things that happen around here.*

When Dena was younger, her older brother Jack slept in the bedroom downstairs on the other side of the kitchen. One night, he heard whistling outside. A couple of nights later, the whistling had turned into rocks and twigs being thrown at the window. He became so angry that he decided to find out what was going on. He opened the back door and ran out, only to see a small, dark, hairy shape melt into the woods. Weeks later, Marvin got home late and found a man-like figure running down the stairs and out the front door. For a while, they stopped hearing the whistling. But another night, when Marvin heard some noises at the back door and opened it, he was completely spooked by what he saw—a little person completely covered with hair. Around the same time, Jack had gone hiking in the woods and, turning a corner, had bumped right into one of the little people. Both screamed and ran for their lives.

I know they are telling me these stories to scare me. Fathers and mothers have told such tales in Indian Valley for hundreds of years. I'd already read about the whuptoli, a half-man half-fish creature that is said by many of the older Maidu to live in these parts. They say that when walking in the woods, you might see a baby floating in the river and feel compelled to go toward it. Don't! Just as you reach your hands out, it will disappear and instead a whuptoli will drag you into the water and drown you.

DENA'S DAD WANTS TO TRAVEL in time and through space. He imagines being teleported off this planet before he dies. They say that when he was a child, he would scare his parents because he talked to spirits around the house that none of the adults could see. When we leave, the road to Shim's Flat flickers in front of our car, the only source of light for miles in the summer night. When we stop, our car brightens the slight bend of the river, and I look closely at the many trees stretching endlessly into the receding darkness. I see nothing. We fall asleep, drinking Wild Turkey and talking about how much is unwritten, how America has and continues to lose itself every day by the death of those who can still remember. Our fire lights the mountain ridge that narrows the sky, and I keep looking for something to jump out of its silence into the world of our voices.

I have watched you from this side of the river ever since you banished me. When I was young, you looked to me as a keeper of your past. In my old age, you turned your back, poisoning your body with white man's medicine, fishing gold from the river instead of trout. Do you remember how you used to run against each other for me, so I could give one of you my spirit? I did the only thing I could do, I turned myself against you.

I wake up surrounded by down feathers and sand. An ember has burnt a hole in my sleeping bag, and I see my friends in the river. They say there is something on the other side of the river I have to see. Amongst mating butterflies and dead butterfly wings, someone has sculpted two faces out of the blackish mud. Their sandy eyes had watched us all night. Two butterflies cling to each other on the owl-like nose of one of the faces, while the rest circle in the periphery of their love.

We move to the back of the room, where there is a pit surrounded by muggu. I get up and place the camera in a nearby corner. The pit is for a fire, and Chandra drops a wadded piece of newspaper into the twigs at the bottom. The flames leap up. The pujaris begin their song again. They will throw rice, ghee, and the occasional stick into the fire for the next couple of hours, as will I, singing "Rama, Rama" with each toss. The flame rises higher until it is as tall as the people who sit around it. Every couple of minutes, I turn around and look at the camera. I'm not used to having it behind me. I hope it is far enough away so it's not coated by a thin layer of ghee and smoke, like the stone surfaces around the pit. I worry to pass the time. I see my tea kettle at home in Los Angeles, its stainless steel surface marred by grease from a year of sitting on the back burner. I remember how dust, embedded in the grease, left a furry residue on my fingers when I touched it. I imagine my camera, like the kettle, suffering the fate of neglected, forgotten objects. In the back room, Chandra's mother rocks his baby back and forth in a cloth swing, lulling him into a deep sleep. One of the pujaris throws a flat piece of dung into the pit. I get up. Switch the tape. Check its dull silver surface.

WE WATCH UNTIL THE SUN RISES in the sky. The day before, Farrell and the elders had blessed the earth, dug out a fire pit, lit a small fire. It can't die out, so is circled by spirit watchers and living watchers, stone watchers and us. The stones around the fire keep it safe. If they fall in, we are to fish them out from the east and bless the fire with a bit of tobacco from our cigarettes from the west. In the early morning, I am wide awake and talking to a young kid, still in high school, out of juvy, who lives with Farrell's parents. It is his first year as a singer, one of the young men who lead the tribe in the Bear Dance. During the gambling games, I hear him chant with the others in languages now scarce but once the only words spoken on this coast. The gambling songs are from different tribes— Paiute, Pomo, or Miwok—not necessarily their own, but now theirs to be kept alive and sung. The songs were written to mesmerize the opposing team; their cadence and rhythm create an aural shield behind which the players hide bones in their hands, passing them back and forth between one another. When their opponents think they know, or when the song ends, they have to guess who has the bones. If they are right, sticks are thrown in the middle by the singing team, and the opposing team begins their song. A young girl with straight black hair steals the games with her stone-like gaze, never letting on that she holds the bones in the smallest of hands.

DURING THE DANCE, a lady on a horse snaps a few photos before we can ask her to stop. The Bear Dance can't be photographed or videotaped. What will she do with those pictures she's galloped away with? Some of us joke that it's like cowboys and Indians all over again. In the photo, she would see a group of people standing in a circle with wormwood stalks in their hands. But the Maidu song Farrell and his brothers were singing would be silent. The photo could not show how we used our wormwood stalks to beat the bear who ran inside the circle. How the children laughed when the bear brushed by, snorting.

His eyes, white and red, showed veins crossing.

His heart beat fast as we turned.

Below blue mayflies.

MATT, MY FRIEND WHO moved to Plumas County when he was 18, drives us around the edge of the state park. He checks its perimeter every night during the summer when he works here as a park ranger; in the winter, he works at the mill. His headlights beam across ridges and down valleys; they illuminate a path through the trees. *Have you ever seen a glory hole, Amar?* He booms. He takes me to a large mouth in the earth. *A glory hole is an old mine shaft that fills up with water.* In the dark, the hole shimmers. Back at the campsite, I drink with my friends and pass out next to the fire. I wake in the middle of the night to stars and trees.

When I open my eyes again, it is still night. The lights in the pine are still there. But so is a bear. It's a foot away from my face and looking right at me. I curse the bag of trail mix and jar of peanut butter at my feet; I had turned my sleeping bag into a beacon. I close my eyes and think of what Farrell told us after my first Bear Dance. *When Worldmaker made the maidum, he gathered all the animals of the forest together and told them, "These are my people, I have made them. They will live here in the forest, and you must live peacefully with them." Of all the animals, Bear and Rattlesnake were the most rebellious. "What made the others so special?" they thought. "Why should we share what we had to ourselves? We will do whatever we feel like"—that is what they thought to themselves...*

Farrell didn't like people taking Maidu stories. They're part of a ceremony, like this one, which is a part of the dance. As I lie in the forest with my eyes shut tight, waiting, I remember what he told me at the end of the ritual. The dance will protect us until next year. It's part of an ancient agreement they once made with Worldmaker. I open my eyes—*I could be dreaming*—but the bear is even closer than before. I thank each breath for quietly persisting. In the old fire circles, they knew warriors came back as bears. The bear of the dance would speak to people in their dreams because he was no different. All around us, voices press us to stand still.

I hear a snap. Through the opening of my sleeping bag, I see the bear on his hind legs. He grabs at a tree. He shakes its shadows.

BETWEEN THE LAKE and Big Meadow sleeps a giant. Long ago, he walked the earth measuring the depths of lakes and streams, but after this particular lake, he became so tired that he fell into a deep sleep and never awakened. If you look at Keddie Ridge, you can discern the outline of his sleeping body. He will open his eyes again, the elders say, and then our time in the mountains will come to an end.

They ask me to lie prostrate on the ground next to the fire, my head facing the base of the two serpents. It is beyond bowing. It is my whole body laid out on the ground. I wouldn't be here if it wasn't for my mother. Back in America, her health is getting better. When my mother first began having problems with her health, Ammamma consulted Sharma, and what he had seen was frightening. He said an atma was draining my mother of her life by eating away at her spirit. It belonged to that place in Benicia. He said it had killed four people so far. It had grown strong like the land, like the windy hill near the lake that was its home. It had been there from long before, from a time we had no record of, no maps, no narratives.

The American grain is a hollow trunk. Only the outer rings remain. We cut away what doesn't belong. Our methods, our mechanical eyes and surgical hands, treat symptoms because origins overwhelm us.

When our house was built, part of a new American suburb, one of many, it moved in. It didn't choose our house because of the maroon carpet or the black and white linoleum. It was attracted to my mother. That was why we had to move.

A FRIEND OF THE FAMILY from the Philippines is the first to see him in the corner of the study. She learned her native form of shamanism from her grandmother in Sacramento. She tells my mother she saw a tall dark man with long hair in the corner of my room. They share notes. He is the spirit from the old house. She offers to get rid of him. They search through my books, looking for an object that could have brought the atma from Benicia over to American Canyon.

Sharma doesn't understand how the atma followed my mother. He asks for a picture of the room. He goes into meditation. The atma is weaker than before. The corner is the only place in the house he can reside. He loves her enough to confine himself between the bookshelf and the wall. He is weak enough for Sharma to exorcise. He warns my mother that her health will worsen over the next couple of weeks as it grows desperate. A month later, Ammamma sees a young girl in the corner. As it grows weaker, it changes form. Each one of its forms is one of the souls it has killed. Soon, Sharma says, it will disappear.

I AM LIVING in Southern California without my books. In West Hollywood, where people seem to have stepped out of the pages of a glossy fashion magazine, I long to see a dusty back cover photo of a lazy-eyed poet or writer needing a haircut. That winter, I drive up to American Canyon, knowing I will come back with arms full of disregard for image, for surface.

They look the same as when I had left them in my parent's study in the new house, except that some have pushed their assigned bookends and are now leaning askew, even bending a little. I reach into the corner of the room to turn on a small lamp to read by; I don't like the track lights sunk into the ceiling. On the carpet, between the end of the bookshelf and the green wall, lies a strange assortment of agate, wire, and crystal.

That night, after dinner, I ask my mother about it. Her eyes are circled in shade like before, when we lived in the old house. *Do you have anything in the study you picked up off the street? Anything you don't know where it came from?*

I think of the wild irises I had shelved in an acid-free archival envelope next to my copy of Mina Loy's *Lunar Baedecker*. When I worked at a rare books library, they had fallen out of a pamphlet from the French revolution. I imagined a French countryside with a woman pressing them into its pages. Two weeks after, while the circulation librarian was on vacation, her substitute told me not to come back to work. We had never gotten along. I took some irises with me.

No, I replied. *Why?*

WE PUT COCONUTS in every corner with kum kum and pasupu and dried lemons. My mother draws in white chalk on the cement walkway that leads up to the front door—curving flowers and dripping leaves, circles and waves.

Her seer, the Brahmin who twinkles his nose when he talks to God, says she can start her life again in this house. This morning, she can step over the threshold. God has a room in the center. He faces east. When she prays, she sees the sun through the windows.

I have waited for years. Each of our rooms are in the places we have adhered to for generations. The first night we will sleep on the floor, after an afternoon of blessing. The second night we will sleep in beds, our heads facing south.

My father lost the persimmon tree and the cherry beside it, the green fig and the French prune he had planted so long ago; I have lost the rosemary I planted around my roses.

The first time my health failed, it was the water I drank from a stream; the second time, no one knew why. I don't sleep for that long, and I never eat outside. My insides are swollen and bleed. I pray instead; some things are not meant to be lost. I listen to my mother who has come to take care of me. Not everything is blood, is my insides. I believe this. I have faith.

I have faith. My loss is her peace of mind. When the rooms around us are the way they should be, as they are now, and God sees what he should, I feel the air circle around me. That never happened before. I see your smile, watch your energy return. You tell me Yama is in the south.

EVERY IMAGE of Subrahmanya Swami is different. He has one wife at one temple, two at another. He rests upon a peacock and holds a trident. His father placed him at the front of the heavenly army. To be one of his followers is to give. To give strictly, to give with austerity.

I know that you do my penance. All of my fathers and uncles are named after him, except me. You tell me to remember the mantra given by the sadhu in the Himalayas, the green-eyed man from Kolkata who spoke French and lived outside the temple steps, a chillum at his feet. In your eyes, his gift was no small one.

I have waited for years. When you were young, I left you with my mother, who took you to sing every day with the old ladies in town by the temple. I know you learned. I learned from my grandmother.

THAT AFTERNOON, the priest arrives. He sets up a pyre on top of a blue hospital gown, and with ghee and fire, begins blessing. When the sirens wail, there is a cloud of smoke around him and a panic of open doors and windows, a fanning of smoke away from the ceiling and desperate jumps from folding chairs at battery chambers. We turn off the fire alarms at the fuse box, but they run on batteries as well, and a house full of Indians is not tall enough to reach a house full of alarms. It's at that moment that we are saved by a tall telephone repairman who asks, *Are you Hindu?*

Patient, you wear the sari with an orange sun that bursts over a rose field that I bought you after shaving my head at Palani and giving all my hair to the temple. I do what a child can. I climbed up a round rock that rose hundreds of feet up, and a baby elephant blessed my naked head with his curled trunk. Around us, women without children covered the pillars with butter, hoping to have one.

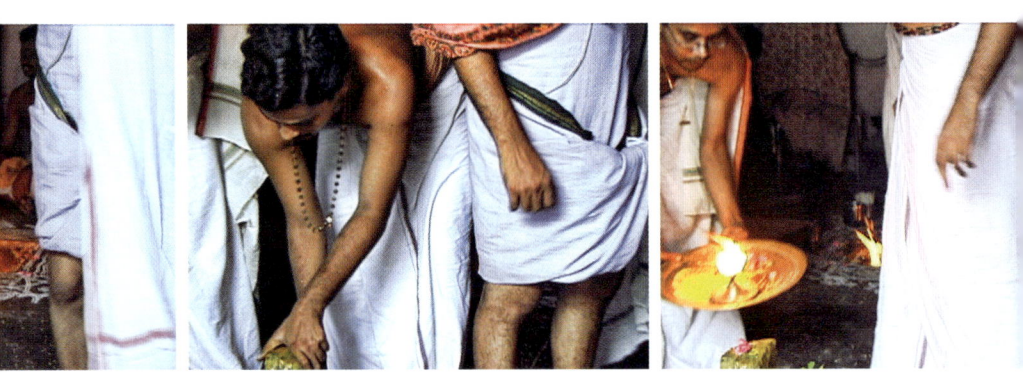

Chandra puts the snakes in a bucket, then hands me a vessel, one of the planets around the sun. Underneath the navagrahas I see white rice. A pujari is picking it up by the handful and placing it in a wicker basket to be used again after it has been shaken clean. I pour water from each planet onto the snakes, then honey, then milk. A bell rings constantly, filling the small room with clangs and oscillations. I pour the water out of the sun. Finish their bath. They are unadorned. The red and yellow from the ritual leaves no trace. They glisten like rocks in a stream.

THE ATMA is what we have forgotten. He confuses us with maya. His body is buried beneath the earth under our concrete. He won't leave until addressed. Did he die in the hills around the lake when he fled from the Spaniards? Did he wander, hoping to be called by name, but no one knew it? Like a wild iris, he calls forth the image of a landscape devoid of houses, cars, and freeways. He is residue, the remainder left over after the galley landed. Chasing the memory of feathers in the river, he walks without rest. He visits our homes in horror. Remembers his village in flames and the song that came out of him.

We never appeased him. We didn't know his name. Had no remedy, no cure, for history. We made him go into remission. Covered the corner with rock. Will he come back, like a naga dosham?

Genes come to us without a salve, are past modification, are inscribed in our bodies. Medicine, the kind symbolized by the caduecus, treats symptoms. Within its narrative, the last solution for ulcerative colitis is to remove the colon and the disease within it. Passed from generation to generation in our genes, it hopes the human genome project will decipher it. The inside of a leaf. Will we understand what we have taken so long to map?

Sharma treats narratives. The ayurvedic and homeopathic methods my mother follows treat her body.

One morning, an atma will talk to me. It will tell me the story of war. The death that follows. The spirits that remain.

Fires.

Wild irises sown in the desert.

Tainted water and sand.

(HOURS) : (MINUTES) : (SECONDS) : (FRAMES)

I turn off the video camera and pack it away. Chandra applies white, then yellow pasupu and red kum kum to the snakes. They wear the powder like clothes. The rest of the pujaris have left, slipping out during the past ten minutes. They are headed to the next ritual, or home to sleep. I follow Chandra out the door, snakes cradled in my arm. Ravi follows. We round the corner and approach the wide arch below one of the gopurams of the temple. Ravi takes our sandals to a booth down the street and checks them in like coats. I step over the threshold. A stream of water rushes over the worn yellow stone under my feet. It cleans away the dirt of the road.

THEY SAY THAT when you were young, you were raised by your grandmother. Your face was like the moon and you wove fresh jasmine into your hair. When she died, you locked yourself in your room all day. Did you learn your patience from her, from holding her old hand as the two of you walked to bathe by the reservoir at the outskirts of town before you went to the temple? Or did you learn it from her absence, when you moved here, where there is no temple to walk to?

In each of us lies a prayer that rests on a blue hospital gown.

In each of us there is a temple that rings its bells.

This is what you have raised, have given. And when I move, and you call, the answer has always been yes. I sleep with my head facing south. I am not ready to look at death in the morning.

(HOURS) : (MINUTES) : (SECONDS) : (FRAMES)

I will carry the snakes, who weigh about 40 pounds, three times around the inner courtyard. All around us, pilgrims will be taking baths in one of the twenty-one different tirthams, each with its own taste and specific malady that it cures. Ravi will tell me the hallway is the longest pillared hall in all of India. It will take a long time. At the end of the hall, I will see an elephant bless devotees for money. I will be afraid of dropping the snakes, which would cause a disaster. After my rounds, I will enter the temple devoted to Parvathi. Outside the shrine will be thousands of carved snakes, stacked up to the ceiling, with new rows growing in height in front of old ones. Each will have a date. Below that, initials. Those dates will stretch back into the past for thousands of years. One of them will be today.

NOTES

7   *In every culture*: from the poem "The Riddle of Bowing" which, according to Lew Welch, is one of the "first American Koans. They are Koans for beginners...": Lew Welch, *Ring of Bone* (San Francisco: Grey Fox Press, 1994), pp. 126–127.

KARMA

12   The *Thirukkural*, or *Kural*, is an epic poem written by the Tamil poet Thiruvalluvar during the 1st century A.D. One of the most important pieces of Tamil literature, it is composed of 1330 rhyming couplets, or aphorisms. Known as the Tamil Veda, it has been translated into 37 languages.

16   *More than a thousand years ago in the Dandak forest*: See the Tamil translation of the Ramayana by P.S. Sundaram, *The Kamba Ramayanam*. This version, written by the 12th century son of a temple drummer named Kamban, differs from Valmiki's in that the reader never forgets that Rama is a God, and that Ravana, though flawed, is a heroic figure. *The Kamba Ramayana*, tr. P.S. Sundaram (New Delhi: Penguin Books India, 2002), pp. 136–140.

    Would he[Ravana] have abducted her if he had remembered the curse?: The story of Vedavathi is found in the seventeenth section of the Uttara Kanda, a section of the Ramayana that is often excised from English translations. J. Muir, *Original Sanskrit Texts on the Origin and History of the People of India, Vol 4* (London: Trubner & Company, 1863), pp. 391–392.

    In Ravana's garden, Sitha waited under a Sorrowless Tree: Dramatic characterization of what Hanuman sees in Ravana's garden. In Sanskrit, Ashoka means "without grief," so the Ashoka tree literally means the Sorrowless Tree. *The Kamba Ramayana*, tr. P.S. Sundaram (New Delhi: Penguin Books India, 2002), pp. 268–270.

18   *folded silk cloth. Each piece has a use in the naga prathista that is never arbitrary*: The symbolism of the colored silk cloth used in the naga prathista is explained by Baij Nath in *Hinduism, Ancient and Modern: As Taught in Original Sources and Illustrated in Practical Life* (Lucknow: Methodist Publishing House, 1905), pp. 165–166: "The moon is represented as white like a sankha, produced from

the ocean of milk, and gracing the forehead of Mahadeo; Mars as bright like lightning, a young man armed with a spear, Mercury as dark like the blossom of the Priyangu flower, and blessed with the attribute of serenity; Jupiter as shining like gold, the preceptor of the gods and the rishis, and the intelligence of the three worlds; Venus as resplendent like the thread of the golden lotus, the preceptor of the demons and the teacher of all the Sastras; Sani as possessing a shining body, dark like a blue mountain, and the son of the Sun and the brother of Yama; Rahu as having only half a body possessed of great strength, the destroyer of the light of the sun and the moon, and Ketu as red like the palasa flower and of a fierce aspect."

22   He felt Roy's activism, like her recent protest: As reported by Coomi Kapoor, "Booker winner Roy sent to jail for a day," The Times (London), March 7, 2002.

A weak argument, I thought, considering the billions spent: For the Sardar Sarovar projects alone, the Narmada Bachao Andolan estimates 44,000 crores (1 crore = 10 million rupees). From Arundhati Roy, The Greater Common Good (Bombay: IndiaBook Distributors, 1999), pp. 21-25.

24   The forests were quiet: Rachel Carson, Silent Spring (Boston: Houghton Mifflin Company, 1962), pp. 103-127.

millions would have died from malaria: For a historical background on DDT's use, see: DDT, Silent spring, and the rise of environmentalism: classic texts Ed. by Thomas R. Dunlop (Seattle: University of Washington Press, 2008), pp. i-xi.

26   The city within its walls had once glittered from the trade of diamonds, giving birth to the Koh-i-Noor, the Hope, and the Orloff: Many noted diamonds, such as the ones mentioned here, were discovered in the Kollur Mine in the Guntur district of Andhra. For an interesting history of some of India's gems, see Katherine Prior & John Adamson, Maharajas' Jewels (Paris: Éditions Assouline, 2000).

His genes had come together to produce his hand: see Roger E. Stevenson & Judith G. Hall, Human malformations and related anomalies (Oxford: Oxford University Press, 2006), pp. 937-940.

27-9   There is a scientific explanation: Interview with Ganesh documented by video on July 5th-6th, 2003, in Ganesh's house in Rishikesh, Uttarakhand, India.

32 *one with Sridevi and Kamal Hassan*: *Sadma*, directed by Balu Mahendra (Bombay: N.C. Sippy & Hrishikesh Mukherjee, 1983).

33 *He used to hunt tigers*: One of the last vestiges of "princely" and colonial habits. "The Big Game Diary of Sadul Singh, Maharajkumar of Bikaner, privately printed in 1936, catalogued his bags over a quarter of a century. In this time, he had ranged far beyond the confines of his desert kingdom in western Rajasthan to shoot tigers in the forested hills of central India, lions in the dry teak jungle of Saurashtra, leopards in Bharatpur and wild buffalo in the Nepal tarai." M. Rangarajan, *India's Wildlife History* (Delhi: Permanent Black, 2001), pp. 35-37, 94-98.

35 *At the back of the shrine*: In Wilber Theodore Elmore's dissertation on the local and village deities of Southern India, he recounts one of the possible origin stories of Podilamma—"Some Sudra farmers lived in a hamlet at some distance from the present village of Podili. One day they were treading out the grain with the oxen in a distant field. Their sister was to bring them the midday meal. On the way in a lonely place she met a man. She put down her basket and was late in arriving with the food. When she arrived, her brothers caught her and threw her beneath the feet of the oxen, for they had been watching her while she came, and believed her to be guilty.

The girl, evidently killed, disappeared under the feet of the cattle among the sheaves. Later when they removed the straw to winnow the grain they did not find the body, but found a stone. A man standing near became possessed with the spirit of the girl and she spoke through him. She said that she had been unjustly killed, and that they must worship her or great evils would follow. All the people who heard this were terrified, and placing the stone in a desirable place they began its worship.

Podilamma, for such was the name of the girl, had now become a deity and soon became noted for power to cure sickness. A rich man who had some serious illness made a vow to her, and was cured. In payment of his vow he had an image made for Podilamma, but it was hideous and all the people feared it. Then another man fulfilled a vow by having a more beautiful image made, and now both images are in the temple. The older image is of stone and has silver eyes which are kept bright, and with a carefully arranged light glare in such a way as to strike terror to the heart of the worshiper. The newer image is of wood and is gaily clothed." From Wilber Theodore Elmore, *Dravidian Gods in Modern Hinduism*, University Studies of the University of Nebraska, Vol XV, No. 1 (Lincoln: University of Nebraska Department of Political Science and Sociology, 1915), pp. 67-68.

37 *He hands me a chart*: Otherwise known as Jyotish. For a basic introduction to vedic astrology, see: Hart Defouw and Robert Svoboda, *Light on Life: An Introduction to the Astrology of India* (Twin Lakes: Lotus Press, 2003).

38 *Before, when there were no roads*: See "Utilizing Traditional Knowledge in Agriculture," delivered by Y. L. Nene at the COMPAS Asian Regional Workshop on Traditional Knowledge Systems and Their Current Relevance and Applications. July 3–5, 2006, Bangalore, India.

40 *chandra, kethu, rahu, shani, shukra*: Note for pg 18, *folded silk cloth. Each piece has a use...*, illustrates some of the symbolism of the navagrahas, or astral deities, and for further information, see Hart Defouw and Robert Svoboda, *Light on Life: An Introduction to the Astrology of India* (Twin Lakes: Lotus Press, 2003).

41 *When the shilpies arrived to this hollow space*: Norris W. Palmer, "Negotiating Hindu Identity in an American Landscape," *Nova Religio: The Journal of Alternative and Emergent Religions*, Volume 10, Issue 1 (Berkeley: University of California Press, 2006), pp. 96–108.

42 *You are purity. Teach this to the others*: See Lise F. Vail, "Unlike a Fool, He Is Not Defiled: Ascetic Purity and Ethics in the Samnyasa Upanisads," *Journal of Religious Ethics*, Volume 30, Issue 3 (Fall 2002), pp. 373–397.

43 *Five hundred years ago, Krishnadevaraya built the gopuram*: S. M. Natesa Sastri, *Tales of Tennalirama (the famous court jester of southern India)* (Madras: G.A. Natesan & Co., 1900), pp. ii–iv. My grandmother's version of the story of Tennalirama [Tenali Ramakrishnayya], or Vikatakavi, was recorded during an interview on July 19, 2003 at her home in Hyderabad, Andhra Pradesh, India. The video was then translated and transcribed with the help of my parents, Subbarao Ravva and Swarnalatha Ravva.

44 *a rain soaked sack on the roof. Inside was a paper trail of property tax documents from the beginning of the century to independence*: In 1902, the French traveler Pierre Loti wrote of the eastern Deccan—"The dryness increases hourly as we penetrate further among the weary sameness of the plains. Rice patches, whose furrows can still be seen, have been destroyed as if by fire...In those that are still alive, watchers—perched on platforms made of branches—are to be seen everywhere trying to scare away the rats and birds that would eat everything; the sun is setting and Hyderabad is at last visible, very white amidst the clouds of dust... The river that flows in a large bed at the foot

of the town is almost dried up and troops of elephants of the same grayish colour as the mud banks are slowly wandering along, trying futilely to bathe and drink" (Davis 160). Mike Davis, in his book *Late Victorian Holocausts* reveals that this scene recounted by Loti was not only the result of the forces of nature, but also exacerbated by the neglect of the "central government under the leadership of Queen Victoria's favorite poet, Lord Lytton," who, even as the country was engulfed in increasing famine and destitution, continued to export India's grain to England (28). At the major ports of Madras and Bombay, callous grain traders routinely dumped grain into the ocean to elevate the price of their product. The colonial apparatus had diligently pursued a systemic erosion of the subcontinent's food security in exchange for cotton production, which was a more profitable commodity then something as useful to local populations as wheat, rice, or millet.

At that time, according to Davis, "The most substantial international aid came not from London but from Topeka: 200,000 bags of grain 'in solidarity with India's farmers' sent by Kansas Populists (American relief organizers were incensed when British Officials in Ajmir promptly taxed the shipment). There was also notable contributions from sympathetic Native American tribes and Black American church groups" (Davis 165). Mike Davis, *Late Victorian Holocausts El Nino Famines and the Making of the Third World* (London: Verso, 2001), pp. 141–175, 25–59.

My grandfather, or Thathayya, was born in a climate of famine. But my great-grandfather also had money to lend, which he did, to farmers who could not afford the British system of taxation that taxed not their grain, but the land they owned. Each year, as the drought continued, more and more of these farmers gave up their land. It occurred to me that my great-grandfather and Thathayya must have developed a problematic relationship with accumulated land that was directly related to the mass mortality, famine, and desperation of local farmers during the late Victorian era. British tax revenues were certainly not applied to this problem, but instead were siphoned out of the town, state, and the country.

My ancestors in Markapur performed the first rite at the temple (according to my grandmother) because they were remembered for numerous instances of forgiving debt as well as for constructing most of the civic institutions in town. Given the cloud of famine and colonial mismanagement, their returning of land, the basis of sustenance in an agricultural community, gave them far more local agency than any other strategy.

45   *two entwined cobras*: For a history of this symbol, see: A. L. Frothingham, "Babylonian Origin of Hermes the Snake-God, and of the Caduceus" *American Journal of Archaeology* Vol. 20, No. 2 (Apr.–Jun., 1916), pp. 175–211. Frothingham notes that "the Kerykeion or caduceus, a pair of snakes wound around a wand or sceptre...[is] the double snake, male and female, the most prolific form of copulation in the animal kingdom" (175).

47   *Prarabdha karma is the fruit of your actions during this life*: Prarabdha is the part of karma responsible for the present body or life, while karma is a combination of both past and present lives. For an extensive explanation of this portion of Sanchita karma, see: Yuvraj Krishnan, *The Doctrine of Karma* (Delhi: Motilal Banarsidass Publishers, 1997), pp. 183–192.

48   *What is your gothram?*: Gothram, or gotra, usually denotes a family with a common ancestor (patrilinear) and represents both endogamous and exogamous marriage rules within one's caste, but a prohibition to marry within the same gotra. In Andhra, one of the founding mythological tales regarding gotra is the story of Kanyaka Parameswari, the Vaishya daughter who refused to marry the Kshatriya king who was infatuated with her beauty. See Joanne Punzo Waghorne, *Diaspora of the Gods: Modern Hindu Temples in an Urban Middle-Class World* (London: Oxford University Press, 2004), pp. 64–67.

      What is your nakshatram? Rohini: It was under the star of Rohini that Bramha set up his sacrificial fires to create his "progeny (or creatures)... and the creatures produced by him remained invariable and constant, like (red) cows (rohini): hence the cow-like nature of Rohini."Julius Eggeling, *The Satapatha-brâhmana. Part I: Books I and II* (New York: Charles Scriber's Sons, 1882), pp. 282–288.

      Amarnath is a cave in the Himalayas: During my research, I found a charming account, full of "heathens, idols, and Mohamadens," of a pilgrimage to Amarnath by the first bishop of Lahore, Thomas French: Reverend Herbert Alfred Birks, *The Life and Correspondence of Thomas Valpy French First Bishop of Lahore Vol. I* (London: John Murray, Albemarle Street, 1895), pp. 289–296.

52   *is a picture of two channels of energy*: Sir John Woodroffe, also known as "Arthur Avalon" was a British Orientalist whose book *The Serpent Power* is the source of many western interpretations of Kundalini yoga practice. According to his translation of the Sanskrit text, Satcakra-nirupana, the Pingala and Ida are: "two Nadis, the pale Ida or Shashi (Moon) and the red Pingala or Mihira (Sun),

which are connected with the alternate breathing from the right to the left nostril and vice versa. The first, which is 'feminine' (Shaktirupa) and the embodiment of nectar (Amritavigraha), is on the left; and the second, which is 'masculine' as being in the nature of Rudra (Raudramika), is on the right. They both indicate Time or Kala, and Sushumna devours Kala. For on that path entry is made into timelessness. The three are also known as Ganga (Ida), Yamuna (Pingala) and Sarasvati (Sushumna), after the names of the three sacred rivers of India." Sir John Woodroffe, *The Serpent Power* (Madras: Ganesh & Company, 2001), pp. 111-112.

MAYA

66   *Rama and his army of monkeys reached the shore of the southern sea. They uprooted mountains*: *The Kamba Ramayana*, tr. P.S. Sundaram (New Delhi: Penguin Books India, 2002), pp. 286-287.

71   *Thousands of years ago, Thataka's heart exploded in the forest*: *The Kamba Ramayana*, tr. P.S. Sundaram (New Delhi: Penguin Books India, 2002), pp. 14-22.

      This was the first time he pierced Maricha's flesh: Mentioned on pg 16, Rama later kills Maricha in the form of a golden deer in the Dandak forest. Though omitted from P.S. Sundaram's version, *The Kamba Ramayana*, this episode is found in Valmiki's version of the Ramayana. *The Ramayana*, tr. William Buck (Berkeley: University of California Press, 1976), pp. 48-51.

84   *I will find out later that a kuladevatha is a local goddess specific to your ancestral home*: This realization is most likely a misunderstanding between me and Pedda Attha. A kuladevatha is a goddess specific to one's family or caste, while the goddess for the town or ancestral home is a grama devatha.

      bits of bone that survive the fire, called flowers: "In contemporary times one major source of obligation is life-cycle rites, particularly rites connected with the dead. Pilgrims come to Haridvar bearing the 'flowers' (bits of bone and ash) from cremation pyres to perform the final death rites by immersing them in the Ganga." *The Hindu World*, ed. Sushil Mittal and Gene Thursby (New York: Routledge, 2004), pp. 491.

85   *My mother says she wants to move into a house that follows vaastu shastra*: For general vaastu design concepts, see Sashikala Ananth, *Vaastu the Classical Indian Science of Architecture and Design* (New Delhi: Penguin Books India, 1998) pp. 45-48, 105-136.

86   *The house has been built according to vaastu, even if accidentally. The housing plan fits most of the rules*: See Sashikala Ananth, *Vaastu the Classical Indian Science of Architecture and Design* (New Delhi: Penguin Books India, 1998), pp. 105–136.

87   *The day Pedda Attha had all the women*: Documented by video on August 5th, 2003, at Pedda Attha's house in Podili, Andhra Pradesh, India.

88   *You can't bargain for your gadde*: The sodi's gadde was videotaped on August 5th, 2003, at Pedda Attha's house in Podili, Andhra Pradesh, India. The video was transcribed and translated with the help of Subbarao Ravva and Swarnalatha Ravva.

98   *Many children are named after Subrahmanya Swami, only the reasons why differ*: Other names for the same god are Guha, Sanmukha, Murugan, Skanda, Kumara, or Kartikeya. Like the variety of reasons people have for naming their children after Subrahmanya Swami, the plethora of his names speaks to the god's mysterious nature, according to Buitenen: "Guha is a God of many names, and the name [Guha] that Duryodhana aptly uses ('the mysterious one') is one of the less common ones. From the point of view of his sonhood he is Kumara, the 'Boy-child'; as son of Rudra he seems to be Skanda, the 'Hopper'; as son of the Pleiads (krttikah) he is Karttikeya; he is also known as Subrahmanya, the 'one of brahminic interests,' as Sanmukha, the 'six-faced one,' and finally as Murugan, the name he bears in the South of India." *The Mahabharata, Volume 2 (Book 2: The Book of Assembly; Book 3: The Book of the Forest)*, tr. and ed. by J. A. Van Buitenen (Chicago: University of Chicago Press, 1975), pp. 205–206.

99   *My mother's mother couldn't have children*: Interview on August 7th, 2003 with Guramma in Podili, Andhra Pradesh, India, at her home. The story was documented on videotape and then later translated from Telugu with the help of Subbarao Ravva and Swarnalatha Ravva.

102   *Slipped into the seams of jackets*: Refers to John Lawrence, the Scottish Presbyterian entrusted with the Koh-i-Noor diamond by the Marquis of Dalhousie. Kevin Rushby, *Chasing the Mountain of Light: Across India on the Trail of the Koh-i-Noor Diamond* (New York: Palgrave/St. Martin's Press, 2000), p. 236.

a distance of twenty-one miles: To be precise, the construction of India's railroads began in 1850—"Finally, on Saturday, April 16, 1853, the first train to run officially in India transported a large group of dignitaries along the 21 miles of track connecting Bombay (modern Mumbai) with Thana (Thane). Newspaper accounts describe a fourteen-carriage train pulled by three engines transporting some 400 people on a day designated as a public holiday...the new engines of change would bring progress and the advancement of what the British saw as their civilizing mission in India." Ian J. Kerr, *Engines of Change: The Railroads That Made India* (Westport: Praeger Publishers, 2007), p. 6.

106   *The news is saturated with terror alerts*: "Casus or casuistry?—Weapons of mass destruction," *The Economist*, May 31, 2003 U.S. Edition.

        the letter in the mail that will infect: William J. Broad, "A Nation Challenged: The Spores; Terror Anthrax Resembles Type Made by U.S." *The New York Times*, December 3, 2001.

        Children in the ruins of tanks: Howard Schneider, "WHO to Study Health Effects of Depleted Uranium in Iraq" *The Washington Post*, March 15, 2001, p. A20.

ATMA

118   *Vents of methane gas jet out of cracks*: Erin Hallissy, "Toxic Nightmare For Homeowners—Experts dig for clues at former Benicia dump," *The San Francisco Chronicle*, November 28, 1994. A more in-depth analysis by Keith G. Wagner reveals that the Braito Landfill, in operation from 1955-1978, was used as a disposal site for many hazardous materials including refinery wastes, sewage sludge, tannery wastes (saturated with hexavalent chromium), and even unidentified materials from the Mare Island Naval Base. The Southampton Company bought the dump in 1977, and after a clean-up operation, began building homes on the former dump site. It turned out that the clean-up was more of a burial of waste than a removal. In 1991, Tom Busfield, an owner of a house on Rose Drive near Blake Court discovered a small depression in his lawn— "The materials in Blake Court were not 'grass clippings' at all, but rather a highly toxic and carcinogenic chemical soup presumably composed of burned tire ash and tannery wastes." Keith G. Wagner, "Homes on Closed Landfills in California: Does the Seller owe a Duty to Disclose?," *Environs Environmental Law and Policy Journal*, Vol. 21, No. 1 (February 1998), pp. 25-31.

119 *In those layers lie cholera and smallpox*: Sherburne Friend Cook, *The Conflict Between the California Indian and White Civilization* (Berkeley: University of California Press, 1976), pp. 209–213.

Upon the rolling hills towards Lake Herman, war broke out between the Spaniards and the People of the West Wind: See J.P. Munro-Fraser, *History of Solano County and Histories of its Cities, Towns, Villages, Churches, Schools, Secret Societies, etc.* (San Francisco: Wood, Alley & Co., 1879), pp. 17–18.

120 *"This is Cemetery Hill, where the Chinese"*: See "Plumas County, California GenWeb Project—Quincy Chinese Cemetery," surveyed by Elizabeth Bullard-Watson, 19 Oct 2003 at the GenWebProject. http://www.cagenweb.com/plumas/ChinCem.htm.

At Promontory Point in 1869, Leland Stanford drove a spike: Rebecca Solnit, *River of Shadows: Eadweard Muybridge and the Technological Wild West* (New York: Viking/Penguin, 2003), pp. 57–58.

More than a century later, an Asian American documentary filmmaker will superimpose her ancestors: Loni Ding, *Ancestors in the Americas: Chinese in the Frontier West, an American Story*. Center for Educational Telecommunications, 60 min. 1998.

121 *They left mounds of discarded shells along the shores of the straits*: Refers to the area of Glen Cove, near Vallejo/Benicia, CA.: Llewellyn L. Loud, "Ethnogeography and Archaeology of the Wiyot Territory," *University of California Publications in American Archaeology and Ethnology*, Vol. 14, No. 3 (December 23, 1918), pp. 347. Loud notes that "In these mounds the stratification is mainly due to the agency of fire and probably results from the practice of cremation of the dead."

the figment of an anthropologist's imagination: "The Wintun were the first of the five groups of Penutian affinity" (351). At least that is what Kroeber claimed to have discovered, armed with his camera in the 1900s, as he was "reconstruct(ing) and present(ing) the scheme within which these people in ancient and more recent times lived their lives" (v). Nonetheless, most of what we know about the Native Americans of California is a result of his research. A. L. Kroeber, *Handbook of the Indians of California* (New York: Dover Publications, 1976).

123 *The first Spanish explorer to the valley saw a river full of feathers*: "...originally named El Rio de las Plumas (the river of the feathers), by Captain Luis A. Arguello,

who led an exploring party up the valley in 1820, and whose attention was attracted by the great number of feathers of wild fowl floating on the surface of the river." Nellie Van de Grift Sanchez, *Spanish and Indian Place Names of California: Their Meaning and Their Romance* (San Francisco: Philopolis Press, 1914), pp. 297–298.

They lay fevered under shade trees near water: Refers to an account by J.J. Warner, quoted in Coyote Man, *The Destruction of the People* (Berkeley: Brother William Press, 1973), p. 104.

In 1830, a sailor returning from the Pacific and another man, a trapper named John Work, carried fever and ague: See Robert T. Boyd, "Another Look at the 'Fever and Ague' of Western Oregon" in *Ethnohistory*, Vol. 22, No. 2 (Spring, 1975), pp. 142–144. Also see William C. Sturtevant, *Handbook of North American Indians* (Washington D.C.: Smithsonian Institute, 1990) pp. 137–143.

worn thin under the collars of the Spanish: For the treatment of Native Americans in California by the Spanish Missionaries, see: David E. Stannard, *American Holocaust: The Conquest of the New World* (Oxford: Oxford University Press, 1992), pp. 138–140.

124　*Coyote Man says back then the people of the Valley*: Coyote Man, *The Destruction of the People* (Berkeley: Brother William Press, 1973), pp. 43–46.

125　*A decade later, Peter Lassen would follow the Pit River*: Sara-Larus Tolley, *Quest for Tribal Acknowledgment: California's Honey Lake Maidus* (Norman: University of Oklahoma Press, 2006), pp. 25–29.

127　*Lake Almanor now glistens where Big Meadow once stretched for miles between the mountains*: See Coyote Man, *The Destruction of the People* (Berkeley: Brother William Press, 1973), pp. 1–4 & 22.

the spring only gives its water to the empty pits of their flooded burial grounds: "The town, its cemetery, and Indian burial grounds were relocated on higher ground just west of their original sites. Dr. Davis recalled that 'when the lake came up it washed all the pits down and in the bottom we found thousands of beads and American money...I would come to the lake every day and see what had washed out of the bank.'" Ibid., p. 37.

128   *Sorties of soldiers from the armory in Benicia followed*: For an account of this, see: Robert F. Heizer, *The Destruction of the California Indians* (Santa Barbara: Peregrine Smith, Inc., 1974), pp. 244–246.

The State paid a total of one million dollars: An extensive report on laws pertaining to California Indians: Kimberly Johnston-Dodds, *Early California Laws and Policies Related to California Indians* (Sacramento: California Research Bureau, California State Library, September 2002), pp. 15–22.

ranging from $5 in Shasta to 25 cents at Honey Lake.: See Clifford E. Trafzer and Joel R. Hyer, *Exterminate Them: Written Accounts of the Murder, Rape, and Slavery of Native Americans During the California Gold Rush, 1848-1868* (East Lansing: Michigan State University Press, 1999), pp. 28–29.

the mercury left behind by the leaching operations of George Hearst: Gray A. Brechin, *Imperial San Francisco: Urban Power, Earthly Ruin* (Berkeley: University of California Press, 1999), pp. 35–68.

130   *"drunken brawlers who wished at a very unreasonable hour to pay their devours to the sleeping beauties of the train."*: As recounted by Marie Potts; see Donald P. Jewell, *Indians of the Feather River* (Menlo Park: Ballena Press, 1987), p. 38.

"Act for the Government and Protection of Indians": Kimberly Johnston-Dodds, *Early California Laws and Policies Related to California Indians* (Sacramento: California Research Bureau, California State Library, September 2002), pp. 5–12.

panned the Hamilton-Bidwell mining claims, now under Lake Oroville: See Donald P. Jewell, *Indians of the Feather River* (Menlo Park: Ballena Press, 1987), p. 75.

"pink rag quarters" they hung on string around their necks: Ibid., p. 77.

131   *These people will crowd us out. We must get out of the way*: Coyote Man, *The Destruction of the People* (Berkeley: Brother William Press, 1973), p. 43.

132   *When Julius Howells envisioned electricity*: Jessica Teisch, "The Drowning of Big Meadows: Nature's Managers in Progressive-Era California," *Environmental History*, Vol. 4, No. 1 (Jan., 1999), p. 35.

Great Western Power approached John's son, Augustus, to sway his neighbors in the meadow: Ibid., pp. 32–53.

GWP brought its first condemnation suit against the Maidu in 1902: Ibid., pp. 41–42.

The entire town was a mile away for a baseball game when a fire torched Prattville to the ground: Ibid., p. 36.

137   *The young maidum who ventures down there begins to dream without the sun; he has passed from our world into another and brought some of that world back with him*: Similar accounts of transformation are recorded by: William F. Shipley, *Maidu Texts and Dictionary* (Berkeley: University of California Press, 1963), pp. 70–73; Edwin Meyer Loeb, *The Western Kuksu Cult, Vol. 33:1* (Berkeley: University of California Press, 1932), p. 200; Roland Burrage Dixon, *The Northern Maidu— Bulletin of the American Museum of Natural History* (New York: Knickerbocker Press, 1905), pp. 278–279.

139   *Maidu medicine men who were nearing death would make a final journey*: Donald P. Jewell, *Indians of the Feather River* (Menlo Park: Ballena Press, 1987), pp. 17–19.

140-4 The stories recounted over these pages were told to me by Dena, Farrell, and Marvin Cunningham in Genesse, CA. in June of 2000.

143   *instead a whuptoli will drag you into the water and drown you*: Another account of the whuptoli can be found in Donald P. Jewell, *Indians of the Feather River* (Menlo Park: Ballena Press, 1987), pp. 23–24.

146   *the players hide bones in their hands, passing them back and forth between one another*: Musical annotations of songs can be found in Frances Densmore, *Music of the Maidu Indians of California* (Los Angeles: Southwest Museum, 1958), pp. 42–43.

148   *drives us around the edge of the state park*: Plumas-Eureka State Park surrounds the old mining town of Johnsville. See Mildred Brooke Hoover, *Historic Spots in California* (Stanford: Stanford University Press, 2002), pp. 286–287.

150   *Between the lake and Big Meadow sleeps a giant*: This particular detail regarding Keddie Ridge is recounted in: *Worldmaker's Trail: An Ancient Trail of the Mountain Maidu Indians* (Quincy: The Plumas National Forest, 1993), pp. 12.

GLOSSARY OF SANSKRIT, TELUGU, AND MAIDU WORDS
IN AMERICAN CANYON

AGNI: The God of Fire.

AKHIL: "Sandalwood" in Tamil.

AMMAMMA: "Maternal grandmother" in Telugu.

ANDHRA PRADESH: Telugu-speaking state in the south east part of India.

ASHOKA: The third monarch of the Indian Mauryan dynasty, who left a large number of edicts inscribed on rocks and pillars in an attempt to establish an empire on the foundation of righteousness.

ASTADIGGAJALU: The name given to the eight poets in Krishnadevaraya's court in the 16th century. It means elephants in eight directions.

ASURAS: A group of power-seeking deities opposed to the devas.

ATTHA: Familial term for "aunt."

BĀVA: Maternal male cousin.

BHAJANS: Religious songs.

BIDI: Tobacco flakes rolled in a dried leaf.

BOTTU: Telugu word for "bindi," a decoration placed between the eyebrows.

BRIHASPATI: Jupiter.

BUDHA: Mercury.

CHAAT: Snacks served at the side of the road from stalls or carts.

CHANDRA: The moon.

CHILLUM: Pipe used to smoke marijuana, tobacco, and bhang combinations.

CHINNA: "Tiny," or "little" in Telugu.

DEVA: God.

DEVI: Goddess.

GADDE: Story.

GANGA: The river Ganges.

GHAT: A broad flight of steps leading down to the bank of a river.

GHEE: Clarified butter.

GODAVARI: A river that flows through central India to the Bay of Bengal.

GOPURAM OR GOPRAM: The tower that crows the entrances of South Indian temples.

GOTHRAM: Geneological term for people descended from the same ancestor. People with the same gothram are not allowed to marry.

HARATHI: A flame, usually made by burning camphor, ghee, or oil.

HOMAM: Hindu ritual using a consecrated fire and offerings to Agni, the god of fire.

HUDESI: The Maidu word for a person who kills without reason.

IDLIS: Fermented black lentils and rice cooked in small mounds, often served for breakfast.

IDĀ: A Yoga-Nadi, or subtle channel of vital energy. The idā is pale, like the moon, and is the embodiment of nectar.

JAGGERY: Telugu word for "molasses."

JAYJAYYA: Means paternal grandfather, but only in the Andhra part of Andhra Pradesh. In Telangana (the other part of Andhra Pradesh), they don't differentiate between maternal and paternal grandfather.

JIVATMA: Physical, mortal beings.

JOWAR: Sorgum.

KALYANA MANDAPAM: Marriage hall.

KAVI: Telugu word that means "poet" as well as "story."

KETHU: A graha, or "planet" without a physical identity in Telugu. In Sanskrit, "kethu" means comet.

KOKONI: "Spirit" or "ghost" in Maidu.

KRISHNADEVARAYA: Emperor of the Vijaynagar empire who ruled from 1509–1529. His empire extended over wide areas of Andhra Pradesh and Karnataka.

KULADEVATHA: A goddess specific to one's family or caste.

KUM KUM: Red powder used in rituals as well as for bottu.

LAKH: Equivalent to 100,000 rupees (Indian currency).

LINGAM: Symbol used for the worship of the Hindu god Shiva.

MAMAYYA: Familial term for maternal uncle.

MANDAPAM: Hall.

MANGALA: Mars.

MASJID: Muslim place of worship.

MAYA: Illusion, the material world, sorcery.

MITA-PAAN: Betel nut wrapped in betel leaves and other ingredients; it is a mild stimulant.

MUGGU: Chalk drawing used to invite good spirits into a house.

NAGA: Telugu word for "snake."

NAKSHATRAM: The star under which a person is born.

NAVAGRAHAS: The nine planets/deities specific to Vedic astrology—surya, chandra, kethu, rahu, shani, shukra, brihaspati, budha, mangala.

NAYANAMMA: Familial term for your paternal grandmother.

PANCHA: A loincloth.

PASUPU: Turmeric powder.

PEDDA: Telugu for "elder" or "big."

PINGALĀ: Parallel to the idā, the pingalā is a Nadi that is red, like the sun, and has the nature of fire.

PONGALI: Rice with moong dal.

PRANA: Life force or vital energy in Sanskrit, prana vayu means sustenance through air.

PRATHISTA: Invoking the consciousness or power of a particular god or deity to reside in an object, statue, icon, or 'murti'. After this rite is performed, worship can then be offered to the murti.

PUJA: Ritual.

PUJARI: Priest.

RAHU: A graha is a planet without a physical identity, but is often depicted by budha (Mercury) riding a lion.

RAKHI: A Hindu celebration of the love and duty between brother and sister.

RAKSHASAS: Demons or evil spirits.

RISHIKESH: In the foothills of the Himalayas, Rishikesh is a holy city in the Dehradun district of Uttarakhand.

ROHINI: The star Alpha Tauri.

SADHU: A saintly person.

SAMBAR: Vegetable stew made with a tamarind based broth.

SARPA: "Snake" in Sanskrit.

SHANI: Saturn.

SHASTRA: System or set of rules.

SHILPIES: Specialized stone-cutters or craftsmen.

SHLOKA: Prayer.

SHUKRA: Venus.

SODI: "Story" in Telugu.

SOKOTI: Small rattle used by Maidu shamans.

SUBRAHMANYA SWAMI: The South Indian name for Karttikeya, the God of War and son of Shiva.

SURYA: The sun.

THATHAYYA: Familial term for your maternal grandfather.

THULSI: Ocimum tenuiflorum, or Holy Basil, is a sacred plant that is considered an avatar of Lakshmi, and is often planted by Hindus in front of their home.

TIRTHAM: A sacred lake, a place of pilgrimage, or body of water at a temple.

TRIVENI GHATS: Steps leading down to the Ganges in Rishikesh for bathing and offering prayers.

VAASTU: Sanskrit word for "house" or "shelter."

VEDAVATHI: A tree of vedas.

VIDYA: Sanskrit for "correct knowledge" or "clarity."

VIZAG: Abbreviation for Vishakapatnam, a north-eastern coastal town in Andhra Pradesh.

WHUPTOLI: Half-man half-fish creature of Maidu legend.

YAMA: The God of Death.

YANTHRAM: Similar to an amulet.

YUGA: "Epoch" or "era" in Sanskrit.

ACKNOWLEDGMENTS

I wish to express my appreciation to the editors of the following publications, where excerpts of American Canyon have previously appeared: *nocturnes*, *(re)view of the literary arts*, *Trepan*, *Drunken Boat*, *Requited*, *[out of nothing]*, *1913 A Journal of Forms*, *The Encyclopedia Project*, and *Parrot #17* (Insert Press).

I would like to thank the Kaya Press editorial board and staff for making *American Canyon* possible.

This book would have never happened if it wasn't for the love, support, hard work, inspiration, and guidance of the following people: Sunyoung Lee, Sean Deyoe, Subbarao Ravva, Swarnalatha Ravva, Vineela Poddatoori, Amina Cain, David Eng, Matt Samuelson, Dena Cunningham, Marvin Cunningham, Joyce Cunningham, Jake Blaufous, Nagendra Rao Tadikamala, Shobha Rao Tadikamala, Pratap Poddatoori, Aruna Poddatoori, Vinny Poddatoori, Subbarathnam Pabbisetty, Jhansi Kavali, Subbarao Kavali, Guramma Ravva, Ramasubbulu Ravva, Rama Pabbisetty, Rama Devi Tadikamala, Jason Brown, Duncan Williams, Katie McGuire, giovanni singleton, José Felipe Alvergue, Douglas Kearney, Lyle Brooks, Janice Lee, Summi Kaipa, Neelanjana Banerjee, Pireeni Sundaralingam, Jen Hofer, Tisa Bryant, Jon Wagner, Janet Sarbanes, Peter Gadol, John D'Agata, Theresa Chavez, Mark Allen, Kate Dollenmayer, Kadet Kuhne, Matias Viegener, Tom Leeser, Christian Nagler, Padraig Riley, Elise Archias, Masha Gutkin, Ishmael Reed, Thom Gunn, Alfred Arteaga, Anne Frost, Emily Abendroth, Amanda Davidson, Fern Alberts, Sandra Doller, Kevin Killian, Colin Dickey, Fanny Howe, Miranda July, Nancy Buchanan, and Varun Soni.

This book is dedicated to the memory of Farrell Cunningham.